PRAISE FOR *WHEN YOU ASK ME WHERE I'M GOING*

"Kaur weaves a captivating narrative that reminds us of what it means to be raw, to be powerful, to be beautifully unique—beautifully human. So many people need this book. I'm one of them." —**KRISTIN CAST**, #1 *New York Times* and #1 *USA Today* bestselling author of the House of Night series, *The Dysasters*, and *The Key*

"Jasmin Kaur's work is divine and essential. Through *When You Ask Me Where I'm Going* she sees you and then hands you the mirror to see yourself. There is a sweet, fierce, and true vulnerability in every piece. Cling to this book; it is honest and it will bring you home to yourself." —**UPILE CHISALA**, author of *soft magic*, *Nectar*, and *A Fire Like You*

"Jasmin Kaur epitomizes a powerful, assertive, and unapologetic voice in her debut. She welcomes us to lean in and listen to the intimacies of her story—to revel in both the beautiful and painful notes of existence. As she challenges expectations and brutal truths, Jasmin offers an insightful commentary on the world from her eyes that is bound to resonate. You will find yourself in awe of the way she so courageously writes about what many cannot find the words to say." —**MADISEN KUHN**, author of *Eighteen Years*, *Please Don't Go Before I Get Better*, and *Almost Home*

"A fierce reminder of the irreplaceable and irrepressible nature of our own voices and the power they hold." —**TRISTA MATEER**, author of *Honeybee*, *The Dogs I Have Kissed*, and *Aphrodite Made Me Do It*

"An emotional journey that will enlighten, inspire, and empower readers everywhere." —**AMANDA LOVELACE**, bestselling author of *the princess saves herself in this one*, *the witch doesn't burn in this one*, and *the mermaid's voice returns in this one*

"A searing and gorgeous debut. This book made me feel seen, but it also educated me—it's sure to provoke many necessary and meaningful conversations." —**JASMINE WARGA**, author of *Other Words for Home* and *My Heart and Other Black Holes*

WHEN YOU ASK ME WHERE I'M GOING

BY jasmin kaur

HARPER
An Imprint of HarperCollins*Publishers*

When You Ask Me Where I'm Going

For information address HarperCollins Children's Books, a division of HarperCollins Publishers, 195 Broadway, New York, NY 10007.

www.epicreads.com

Library of Congress Control Number: 2019941400

ISBN 978-0-06-291261-9 (trade bdg.) —

ISBN 978-0-06-291262-6 (pbk.)

Typography by Jordan Wannemacher

20 21 22 23 24 PC/LSCH 10 9 8 7 6 5 4 3 2 1

First Edition

to ishleen

and all the other kids

who seldom see themselves

in books

there is nothing gentle about these poems.
even the flowers dripping from my tongue

sharpen their edges on glass. douse
themselves in propane. prepare their
petals for war.

contents

skin (n)

the outermost layer of a body. a sheathing. an organ. a protective covering. a composition of dead cells that comprises most of the dust within a home. that which is seen first. that which hides the rest. a wall between the earth and my soft psyche. an unmissable thing. a curious thing. a shameless thing. a migratory thing. an organic human history. a burning building your eyes roam. a neon sign. an altar for worship. the place where we first met. a beacon of light. a blaring siren system. a kind of refuge at the very edge of a cliff.

and what is it about the skin?
it's where they draw all their conclusions.

my skin (and everything carried on it) is the first me you will encounter unless you're meeting my words before you've met my face

if that's the case, i'm excited. it means that this is one of those rare and beautiful moments when everything inside of me is going to matter more than everything outside of me.

this neighborhood is hushed whispers from those who will only graze her perimeter. this neighborhood is clean-cut, harmless houses and the stifled stories they are home to. this neighborhood is a surveillance camera made for children tangled up in something hollow while their parents are tangled up in money for the mortgage. husbands who smile for their wives. wives who cry for their sons. because of their sons. because of their daughters. and sometimes because of their husbands. this neighborhood is an unwanted migration of punjab to the promise of soil fertile enough to replant roots. this neighborhood is twelve hours sifting through berries and hours more hoping that aching backs and hands and minds will one day come to fruition. this neighborhood is a white woman who tells me that i live in a dangerous place but that it should be fine for people like me. this neighborhood shouts. and throbs. and breaks. but she has never failed to plant hope.

call us concrete children
broken by the cracks
in the sidewalk   children
or turned out okay
despite the odds   children

call us unworthy children.
born on the wrong parallel
of the wrong side of the earth   children
call us unteachable immigrant   children
            or angry brown   children
            or your success story   children

or
simply
call us children.
so that for once
that is what we are
allowed to be.

inspired by tupac shakur's
"the rose that grew from concrete"

some boys
break boys who
look just like them
because somewhere
along the line
they were taught that
when they are hurt
someone else
must hurt more

and the cops know
their stories to begin
and end with
bullets escaping guns.
or weed exchanging
hands. or their clothing.
or their skin.

but i've seen what
they tuck behind their
locked-door eyes.
the way their mouths
harden up before they
cry.

ਸਬਰ / *sabar* / patience

some mothers wear patience
far too gracefully.

it is the shawl draped over
her shoulders every time her son
walks out the front door with no
regard for the ones still suffocating
in this house

it is the scarf calmly covering
her head   hiding the black dahlias
on her neck

it is the intricate pashmina wrapped
around her body when i see her catching
tears in cloth or hiding bloodshot eyes
behind the protection of her chuni
or wiping all the sadness away with the
very thing that she refuses to remove.

product recall

in this world
worth is defined by the way
poreless skin stretches across
correctly chiseled bone
by the places where
fat strategically stores itself
by the obedience we hold against
our own heads—safety removed
as we discard all the pieces of us
that do not fit within the plastic mold.

ਪੱਕਾ ਰੰਗ / *pakka rang* / ripened color

when they whisper that
the heat of her mother's womb
must have turned her skin to ash

she laughs
because they cannot see all the god
in a body draped in earth and fire
and gold all at once.

an open letter to south asians

but what if you get dark
is to say that dark bodies don't let light in
is to say that there is something dirty
about the biological makeup of skin
is to say that some people are born clean
and need to keep it that way
is to say that you don't hate black people
but you thank god you weren't born one.

so roop stares into the bathroom mirror and prepares her face for a fistfight. the foundation is two shades too light, so she does her best to smoothly blend it into her neck. her mom walks in and wanders her skin with her eyes. and her grandma walks in and nods. and her aunt walks in and tells her that the guests have arrived. the guests are polite. they talk about the family's health. they talk about the price of houses. they talk about the leadership race. but they don't talk about roop's face. and nothing good or bad is noted of her. and this time, it seems as if the camouflage has worked.

i’m trying to settle into my body
feel comfortable inside its walls
stay long enough to decorate each room
sit at peace within me

i’m trying to come home to myself
                                        i really am

but you underestimate the way   eyes
can knock on doors and break through
windows and tear down foundations
how eyes can whisper and laugh
and scream

you underestimate the way hate
can pull me to tears and push me to leave
once again.

kes (n)

the uncut hair kept by sikhs as a means of
recognizing the divinity within one's natural form.
an expression of love. a sense of freedom from
the ideals of consumeristic and eurocentric beauty

sunday.
you catch the corner of a mirror
and can't help but notice the strand
of hair. always bolder. always louder
than before but you tell yourself that
there are flowers growing from your skin.

monday.
the train is a cacophony of beings.
humans as lost and hopeful as you
and you can't help but weave stories
of their struggles between each stop

but their eyes drown in your sight.

he glares.
you smile back.

tuesday.
you find yourself consumed with glass.
rectangles and squares and prisms and
shards that are always painful no matter
the dullness of the edges.

wednesday.
she turns to you in class. after months
of small talk she musters up the nerve to say

do you mind if i ask you a question?
you nod. you already know what it is.

thursday.
you're trying to hide from glass.
but your body was not made only
to run. what if you slowed your
pace long enough to listen to
your skin?

friday.
you stumble upon a mirror.
but before you can escape you catch
your eye on a glimmer of light.
there is something glowing
just beneath the surface
of the being before you.

saturday.
you crown yourself.
this time taller
this time willfully
you seek all the stories
locked within each
softened layer of cloth
wrapped around your
head.

today, these stories are enough.

sunday.
you encounter flowers
scattered across your skin

for the first time, you stop
to sit among them.

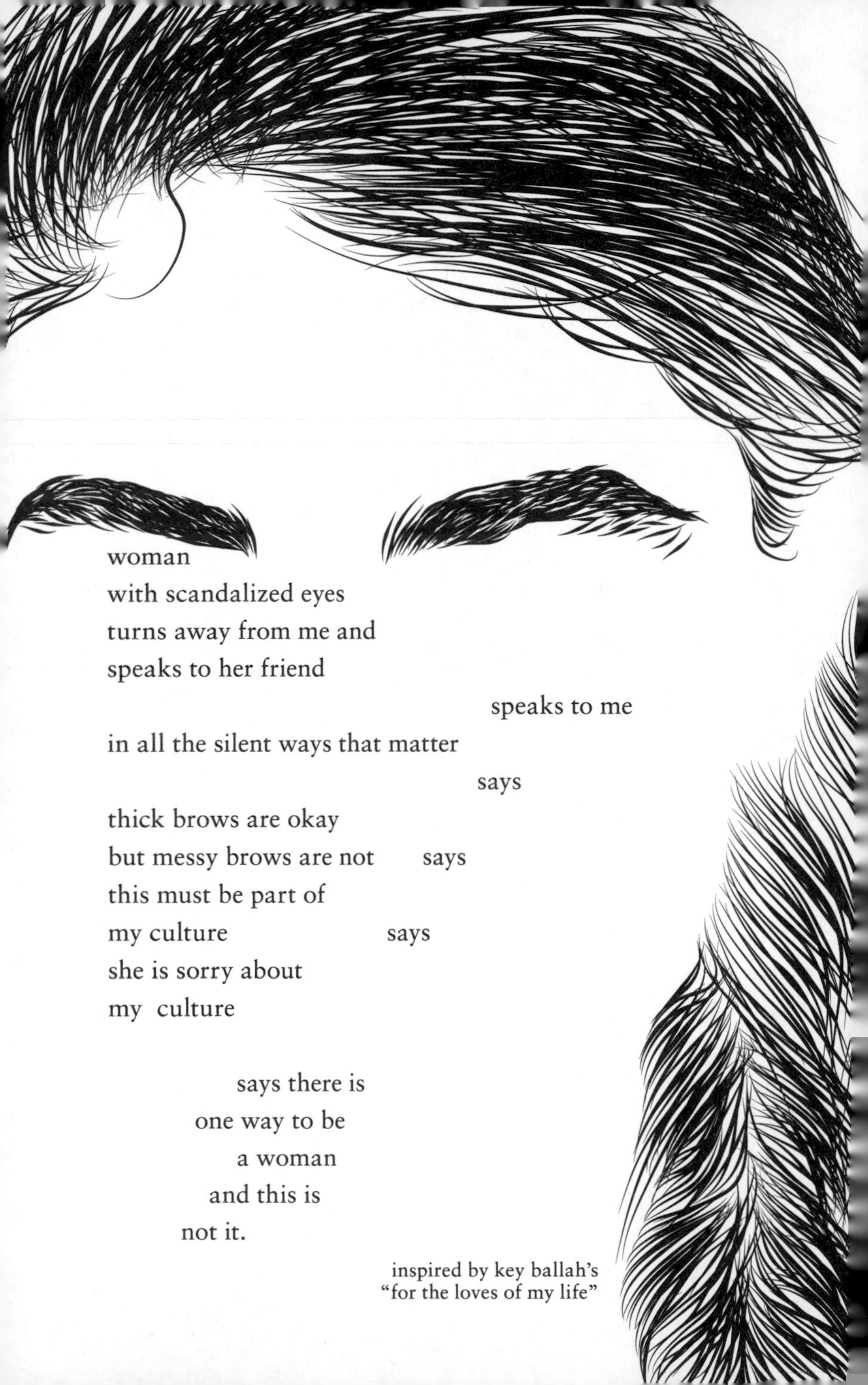

woman
with scandalized eyes
turns away from me and
speaks to her friend

speaks to me

in all the silent ways that matter

says

thick brows are okay
but messy brows are not says
this must be part of
my culture says
she is sorry about
my culture

says there is
one way to be
a woman
and this is
not it.

inspired by key ballah's
"for the loves of my life"

the ideal sikh girl
only radiates grace
across her hairless face

she is born with so little
in need of fixing
that they will stare
deciding whether or not
her form has been altered
until the corner of her eye
catches the heat of
    their   gaze

when they finally realize
that it is only nature
who has been so kind to her
they will no longer hide
the hunger in their eyes
as they inform her that
she is beautiful.

i'm not here to be your example of the good girl
until i'm your warning sign for the wayward one

ਨੂੰਹ / *nooh* / daughter-in-law

her mother repeats a familiar invocation
recites the words that have already gone
stale in her mouth

treat her no differently than you would treat me
remember that they are your family now
their home is your real home
but it is not yours

do not overstep their bounds
or let your tongue get comfortable
they are yours and they are not
they are yours but they will not
love you despite it all

and so she leaves to
not her home.

babygirl
didn't your mother
ever teach you
that when these hips
widen into the earth's arch,
this body will no longer be yours?

you will be baptized into womanhood
by all the eyes that own you.

on trial

girl no older than thirteen
stares up into the eyes
of humanity
and apologizes
for the gaze of men

humanity
no jury to be blinded
by a bleeding heart
remains unconvinced
of her sincerity.

my name is not sheila but i'm wondering if i have the right to a jawani or a life all in which i am not pulled apart hip by hip. in bollywood a woman is meant to remain calm while fifty-three men encircle her with mouths watering just as calm as she must remain in each of these streets where her compliance keeps her alive. *munni badnaam hui* but her attackers still walk the streets honor intact because every single day in the world's largest democracy™ the word *izzat* takes precedence over the testimonies of ninety-five women and god knows how many other whose voices have been stifled.

when durga stepped out into the battlefield her oppressors' heads hanging from her neck i wonder if she was met with respect or whether they viewed her skin as a land that hadn't yet been conquered.

down aisle six
on a shelf that's not too hard to reach
is barbie.

packaged in pretreated plastic
barbie has a propensity for promiscuity
all the features they want of her:
lips full, hips curved, eyes bright

barbie's arms don't bend but
she can get down on her knees
made to please those with
a moment's attention

she is
labeled, branded, and set on display
waiting rigidly for ken to glance
in her direction
trying to fill that hollow space
between molded layers of peach plastic

but can you really blame her?

she didn't place herself
in that box.

they taught her that
hell existed at the curve
of her waist. because the
shape of her body left
boys wanting. tempted
them like apples
hanging from
trees. like fruit that
wanted to be picked.
made their minds wander.
left too much to the imagination.
too little to the imagination.

he taught her that hell existed
in the hourglass of her being
in the small of her back
in the movement of her legs
when he invaded her because
the sin was too tempting
and she prayed for
forgiveness.

boys with microphones
love to talk about queens
love to separate the humans
from the hoes

love to sexualize
the intelligence of women
love to tell you that you are
not like the other women

love to praise women
so women will
want them.

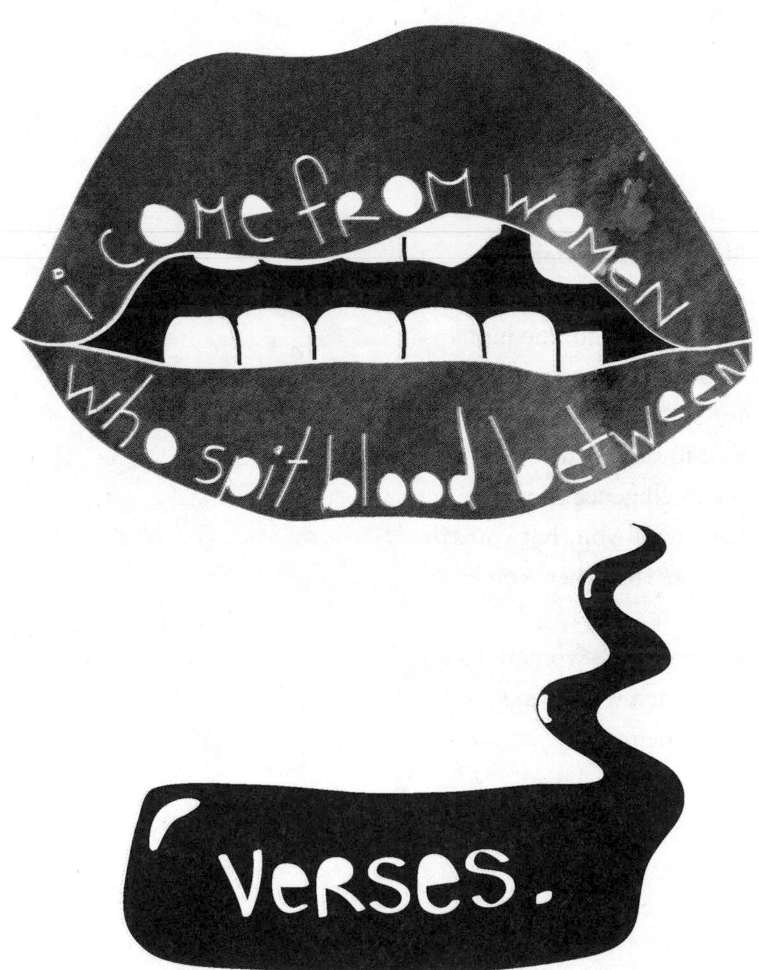
i come from women
who spit blood between
verses.

ਕੋਡ ਸਵਿਚ / *kode-svich* / code-switch

why should my tongue
choke on itself for my
intelligence to be proven?
i will not call my voice colloquial
when yours is always welcome in its natural form.
my words nach between two languages fighting over them.
my thoughts travel the earth before i collect them.
and if they need to be described in a boli that sounds
barbaric to ears that don't know how to hold them
so be it. i will not italicize all the parts of myself
that make no sense to you.

you are the wrong kind of writer. the kind that doesn't always have the right words and seldom has them in the right order. your commas pretend to be periods and your metaphors sometimes spill over the edges of convention. you sit in bookstores cross-legged at the bottom of the shelves. love too many of the books and take none of them home. your lines don't usually fill up the entire page and your english teacher usually fails you for not fleshing out your thoughts. most times, there just aren't enough words. there are enough stories, but there sure as hell aren't enough words. you don't have snap-worthy sentiments about love but you know what it is to fall asleep during a graveyard shift and lay awake for hours waiting for no one to come home. the english is still unkind. still scrapes the bottom of your tongue on its way out and the metal on your pencil still scrapes the paper where the eraser is worn. you tell me all the stories, sitting cross-legged at the bottom of the shelves. you think they will never find their way into the stacks above us unless another hand scribes them. one without so many calluses. one more familiar with poignancy than honesty.

when i was ten years old, i had no idea that chimamanda ngozi adichie would one day describe the danger of a single story   but there was a moment. a definitive moment. when her words hung low in the air in this very desi public-school classroom. when a man much older than us. much more powerful than us. and much paler than the little punjabi faces that looked up at him. was angered by the actions of a few boys in our class. he said

you boys act like this because indo-canadian dads have no manners. because they treat you like little princes. because they have no respect

and when you are ten years old and punjabi you don't talk back to adults. let alone your teacher. but you wonder things that you cannot yet wrap your entire heart around. like   how can he talk about my dad when he's never met my dad before   and   why are we all in trouble
when two boys did something wrong   and
are our families really as bad as he says they are

so you grow up searching for answers between the covers of books and conversations on twitter and your own tongue that begins to grow poems. but some of the questions only become dense and bottomless. a well within you soon overflowing with murky water.   like   what if they call this one story every single story   and   what if they read these words and think they have walked these very same halls   and   can i tell my people what i saw without
a white man interrupting to tell us that he was right

i add myself to the dictionary
set our skin tones to default
remove the wavy red lines under every name
and tear down the borders they built
on each page.

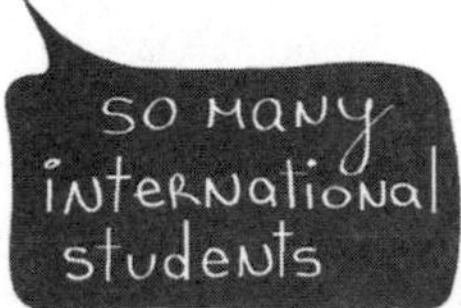

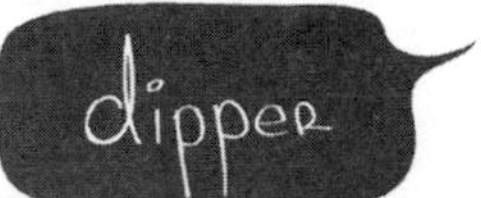

if you love
writing about the
way your tongue has
been stolen from its mother
but cannot see those from
your motherland within you

believe me when i say
that the colonizer has
already strangled and
swallowed you whole.

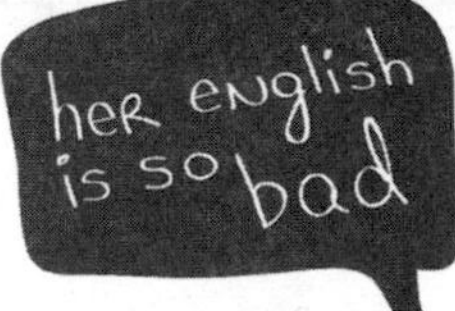

he tells me he doesn't care about politics and i am lost. i am a brown woman born on land stolen, sacrificed and then silenced. i am a brown woman born into a body that turns heads that only house glares. glares that ask me to leave. mouths that spit blood toward my kind. hands and fists and forces that want to push me back to where i come from. while where i come from screams in ways that go unheard. where i come from is buried under blistering earth and burning minds that are set aflame by a state that brings kerosene instead of water when my people are thirsty. where i come from is being dug out of the dried soil by people young enough and old enough to demand more than justice from those who have tried and failed to crush them. he tells me he doesn't care about politics and i wonder if he can see the political boundaries on my body—the conflict zones between my shoulder blades. the border built between my tongue and me. the partition carved into my palms. all the ways in which it is political for me to live.

the sun rises

& israel drags his feet across gaza's chest.
settles across her skin & waits empty-eyed for
it to tear

& a white man sits atop amerikkka & calls
brown skin a furnace. says that we consume
each other in smoke & flame. that it is better
we burn each other to ash than intrude on his
property

& a cop in punjab empties out a cartridge.
cleans it out in a young singh's body & names
it necessity. decides to side with a system that
puts food on the table & bodies in rivers

& a woman floats in space. stares at the earth
as the sun cowers behind it. watches existence
light up in twinkling cities & villages. wishes
humanity could step back to stare at itself.

undocumented

what is purgatory but to meet no place that calls you beloved
to find no earth with arms that embrace you
to swim only in rushing rivers and never rest beneath the sun

where do you go when each floor of the house you built is
on fire & the cold hearted encircle you   bullets loaded in
their mouths demanding that you go back to where you came
from

it's true. we were never welcome here.
those of us with sun-showered skin and
generations of rebellion dancing
beneath our rib cages

not aching to make our struggles romantic
nor to kiss the word *exotic* like a compliment

not simply searching for another way to say
that our legs must stretch & tear to plant feet
in two continents

but instead walking toward a justice
that cannot be commodified.
one that cannot be softened
and sold back to us.

in this body   i am
a work of art that will face unsolicited critique
a wrong answer on a test that i never agreed to take
& a set of rules that have undoubtedly been broken
but i would be lying if i told you that this skin
does not hold me close
                    because in every shade of neon
their disdain and curiosity is drawn to me
and all the while   i glow.

muscle (n)

the tissue responsible for movement. propels action. sets the story of this body in motion. expands and contracts without crumbling. pulls away. pulls in. then fills all this space once again. strengthens when torn. but it hurts. and that can seldom be avoided. when torn. when teaching itself how to heal. it only knows how to fill more of the room than before. listens closely to feeling. to the fluctuating colors i carry. knows its way around my anger and responds in love. in outrage. lets itself be consumed with blood. meets both fight and flight. prepares for the consequences of either one.

but what if muscle doesn't fully heal?

it makes itself heard.

the next time you ask me where i'm going
please recall that i am three parts indecision
and one part reckless abandon
that i have seldom bothered to look back
at the wreckage i've left in my wake and
will never be bothered to master the flames
at my fingertips anyways

i am not your poem.

i was never your brushstroke.
i am not your tragedy
or your failed attempts to find meaning.
i was never an answer to a question
so when you ask me like dawn
if i will rise to your occasion
do not be disappointed when i reply
with the dusk that is all i've ever known.

they say you're angry. with your loudmouth response
to everything. with your mess where they expect
organization. you undo all their seams just to prove you
can do them yourself. greet demands for silence with
rushing water. walk out the doors and over the lines
to remind yourself that you can. coat your knuckles
in brass beneath the skin. meet the feet on your body
with all the shrapnel on your tongue. swallow outrage
and spit it back out. never leave without an answer.
never end without the last word. snap back when you
feel suffocated. always more than necessary. seldom
enough to compensate for that deep dark fear of cages.

scream
so that one day
a hundred years from now
another sister will not have to
dry her tears wondering
where in history
she lost her voice.

tell me how to scream

how do you do that?
scrape me off my words
before you digest them.
water down all the kaur.
all the punjabi. turn identity
into nothing more than caricature.
turn a lineage of empowerment
into a single poet-shaped joke.
how do you do it so easily?
silence the very voices you
claim to celebrate.
pit me against my own poems.
how do you sever my body
from my tongue as you
set it out for display?
maybe   at this point
you should just keep it.

when you are among men
who call your voice the spark
for every wildfire they've set
you begin to soften your words
without meaning to

you call yourself water
and try to douse flames
that have nothing
to do with you.

you ask me to speak my truth in digestible doses
and tell me to lie.
my tongue will not be severed & diced
spread thin across a surface
& seen in segments
for space at the table.

not when this voice could pull the table apart.
repurpose it.
build a raft.
a bridge.
a way forward.

you tell me to take a seat here.
on this pedestal that you have
carefully constructed only to
pull the wooden legs out from
beneath my body when my
mouth no longer forms
the words of your choosing.

you tell me to radiate.
how to radiate. how to glow
beneath the lights and force
my chest to rise and fall as
my voice rises then crawls
to the rhythm of an audience.

you tell me to perform for you.
to turn my feeling into theater
tear open my chest to inspire
fill all the cracks in my voice
with cement because bold
women must hide all their
human.

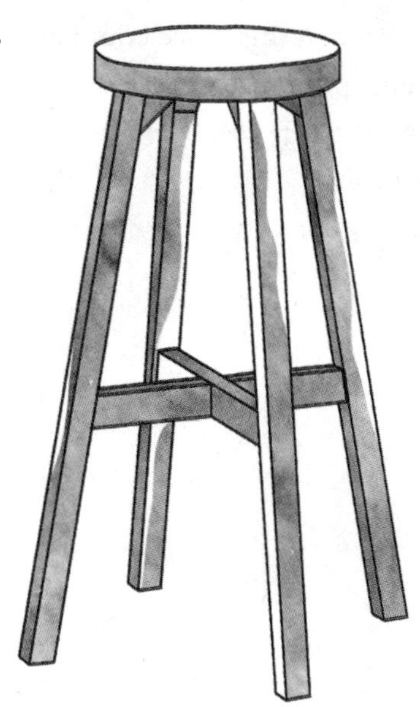

and i show you all the ocean
in my intentions. all the untamed
tides beneath my tongue that will
swallow you before you ever
attempt to master them.

all the floodwater that will find
its way into your microphone.
short-circuit the wiring. burn out
the stage lights and tell you to
go home.

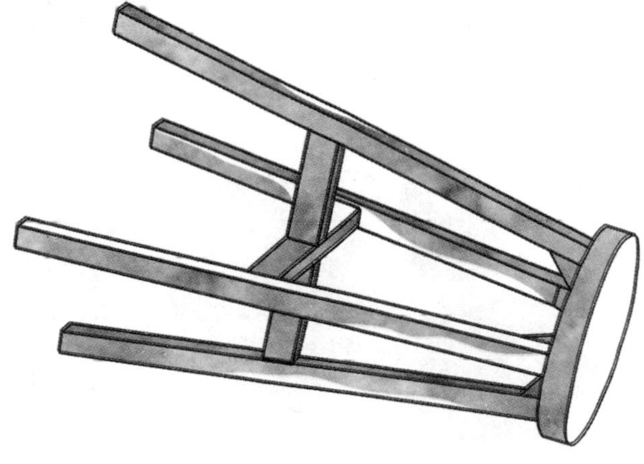

when they throw
the word *feminist*
at you like a fist
against your ribs
like an aged curse
like your mother's shame
pry it from their fingers
and weave it into your tongue
drape it across your skin
or abandon it altogether
but remember that
this weapon is yours
to use however it is
you please.

some of the men
pray for you
prey on you
pray that god will save you
prey that god will break you
pray that they never marry women like you
prey that they tame women like you
pray that their daughters never hear you
prey that their daughters sound nothing like
their mothers

brother
when did you forget
that the walls of
a woman's body
were once a fortress
protecting you from
a world you were
too fragile for?

she has been
defending you
long before you decided
that she has no place
defending you.

am i meant to burn my bones in guilt?
am i meant to douse myself in shame?
am i meant to apologize for the way
you could not make me love my own
oppression?

the violence comes soft and polite
dresses up in a three-piece suit
irons its pants
tucks in its shirt
reads from a teleprompter
shakes your hand
asks about the family
asks for calm and order
law and peace
reaches for your throat
with a stack of papers
suffocates with legislation
pours fuel on the land
ignites with a signature.

i don't know how to smile
through the debate that turns
my humanity into a question.

i don't know how to stand
for a country. for a cloth.
for a border. that fences me
in and keeps me out.

framing

perhaps the real ruler of the world
is marketing

erase a little iraqi girl and call her collateral
blur the details of a black man's face
and say he fits a description
make them feel like they
belong inside a country
and soon they will know
who to push out

it won't take long for people
to believe this border really exists
even if there isn't a wall
to stare at.

i once read somewhere that revolutionaries
withstand torture by recalling the reason
why they resist, so when he asks me his
first question, i level my eyes with his
and translate the stories buried beneath
my skin

where are you from?

eyes still locked into his, i say
my body was birthed upon stolen sto:lo land
stripped not ceded from people who live
and breathe the earth you stand upon in ways
you will never choose to understand.
my mind is severed in five fragments across
a border between the two halves of my self.
a border dug upon my spine stealing feeling
from me and i am nearly certain that punjab
is just as numb as i am.
and my soul. that was shattered and mended.
killed and revived. over and over and over in
a place closer than your own heartbeat.
in the deathlessness of a revolutionary
who taught me that i am you.

dedicated to bibi resham kaur
sexually assaulted and murdered by punjab police
on october 22, 1993

to punjab police

i hope you are haunted
by the watching eyes
of every woman
whose body was invaded
in the name of law and order.

the revolution is working on
her anger-management issues

this time when she is
beaten for speaking out
against her oppressors
she will smile and be
diplomatic about it.
she promises not to escape
from the prison cell again
because she has learned
that the court of law only ever
moves in the favor of justice

she knows this implies
that she is the injustice.

on those velvet black nights, when there is only anger in place of poetry, i will paint the walls with my knuckles. my mourning doesn't know how to sanctify itself. how to dress itself in figurative language and present itself as an aesthetic. the tragedies between these words know how to thunder not only in metaphor.

don't get me wrong.
forgiveness and i are well acquainted

but just because she had good intentions
it doesn't mean she ever kept me safe.

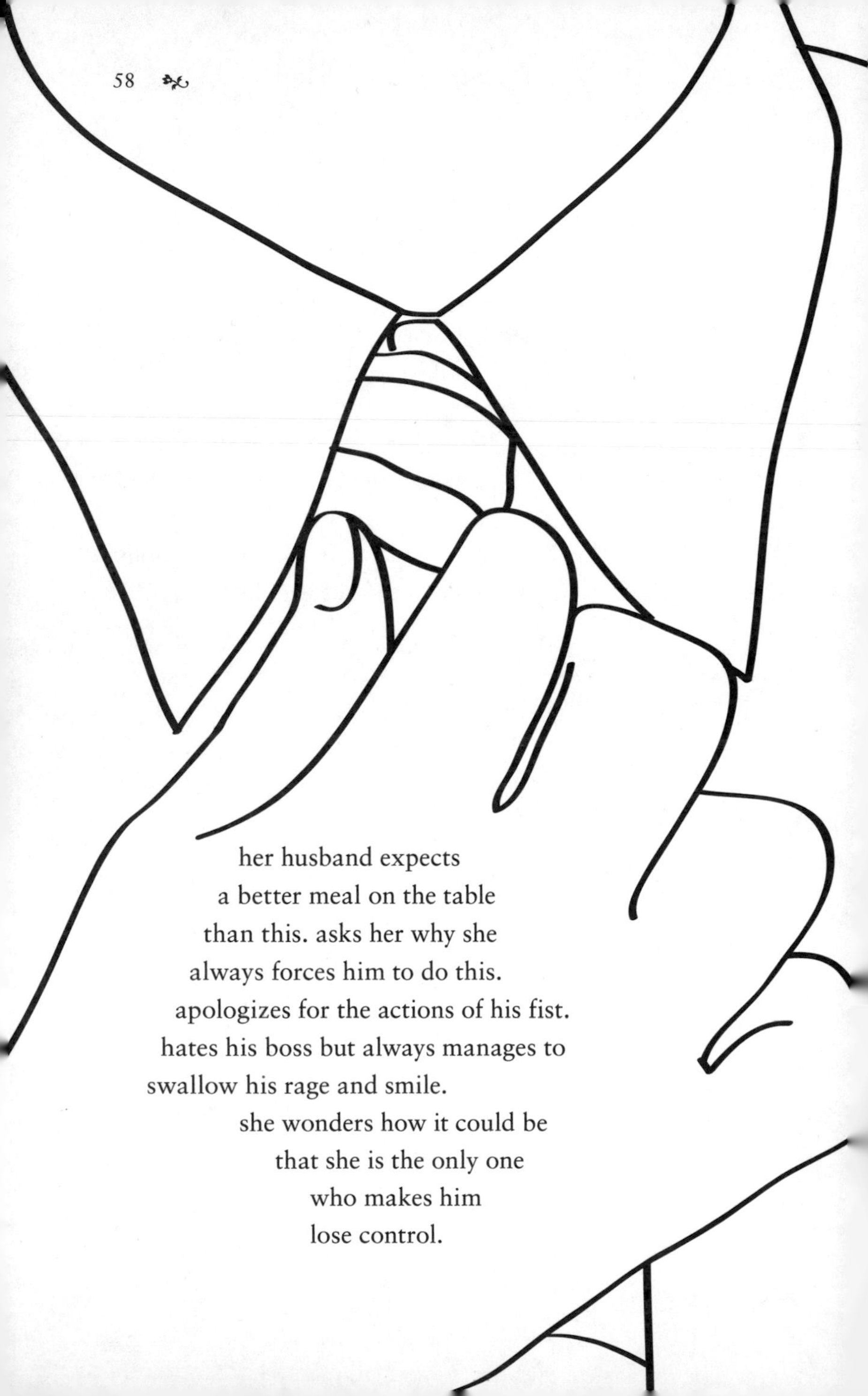

her husband expects
a better meal on the table
than this. asks her why she
always forces him to do this.
apologizes for the actions of his fist.
hates his boss but always manages to
swallow his rage and smile.
she wonders how it could be
that she is the only one
who makes him
lose control.

i still have nightmares about the rage.
it finds me
in my stillest dreams
where gentle wind slips through grass
to graze my skin

and charges toward me
like an unforgiving storm.
skies churn to ash
sun disintegrates below horizon
and i am eight years old
all over again.

he built lego planes that shot lightning bolts at bad guys
collected comic books that no one was allowed to touch
dug carrots out of the dirt before they were ready
made kids jealous with his metal-spiraled beyblades
rode his bike in circles around his sister to make her laugh
wore softness on his skin until the age of eight
left lego scattered across the carpet like a maze
hid behind mom when dad stepped on the lego
reread his comic books to drown out all the noise
dug holes to a place where dads weren't allowed
smashed the beyblades on the cement when he was mad
crashed his bike into the trash cans and tried not to cry
struggled to keep all the softness stuffed in his pockets.

middle school

sometimes in the locker room
he would forget to
cover up the marks

i fell on the sidewalk
was boxing with my cousin
tripped when i was walking down the stairs

but that day in the back field
when he ran out of stories
he made me vow to never
open my mouth
because social workers
were only good at
messing everything up.

instead of calling for help
we learned to carry the weight
of all these secrets on our shoulders
absorbing pressure in glass-jar bodies
hoping no one would notice.

when he begged her to go

we are made to believe
that the real violence
occurs once we leave.
that the swollen lips
and aching bruises
and voices ringing in our ears
are just a warm-up
for the pain that life
would place
on our shoulders
if we were to run

and it is the seed
of this single thought
planted ever so carefully
that sprouts and flourishes
growing large and tangled
around every crevice of my mind
that gently wraps itself over my eyes
and tells me how it would be
so much easier

just to stay

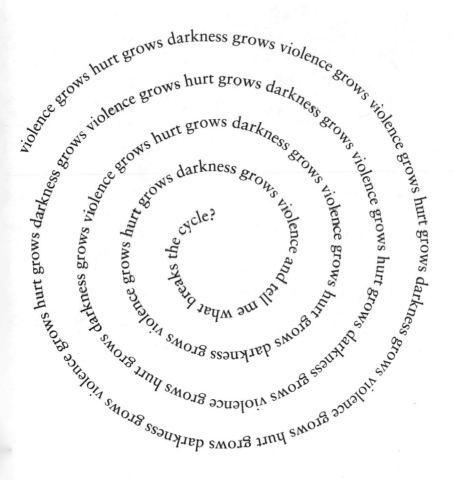

violence grows hurt grows darkness grows violence grows violence grows hurt grows darkness grows violence grows hurt grows darkness grows violence grows hurt grows darkness grows violence grows hurt grows darkness grows violence grows hurt grows darkness grows violence grows hurt grows darkness grows violence grows hurt grows darkness grows violence grows hurt grows darkness grows violence grows hurt grows darkness grows violence and tell me what breaks the cycle?

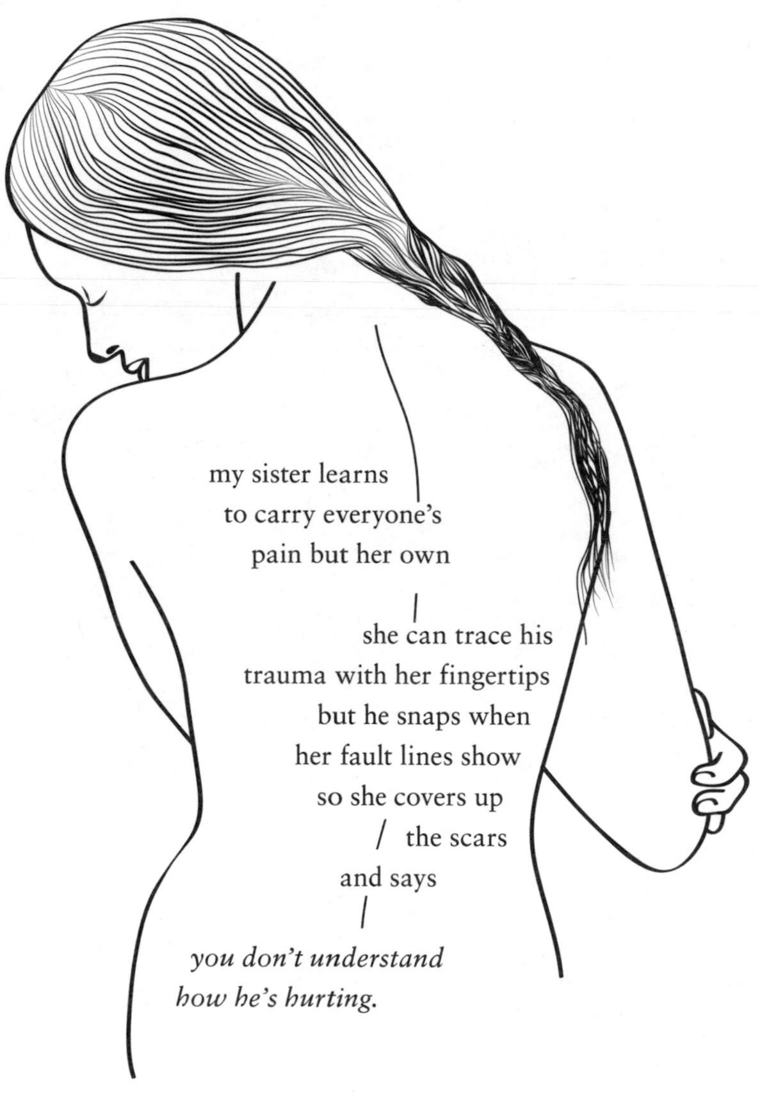

my sister learns
to carry everyone's
pain but her own

she can trace his
trauma with her fingertips
but he snaps when
her fault lines show
so she covers up
the scars
and says

you don't understand
how he's hurting.

in case you were ever told otherwise

allow me to make this as clear as distilled water

it is never your fault.

their hands are only their hands. they are not trip wire
that can be set off by your tongue. or your actions.
or your mistakes.

their bodies are only their bodies. they do not disobey
their owners or forget to follow orders.

their decisions are only their decisions.
you did not make them do this.

you are not the moon
and the tides of my
well-being will not
be pulled by your
every mood

you are not the sun
and i will not move
helplessly to the rhythm
of your burning orbit.

on gaslighting

he is an artist
skilled in the craft of running
roughened knuckles against skin
and turning the impact into her own
guilt

his inspiration arises from a range
of sources but most often he cites
alcohol and her mouth.

he reaches for another glass
as if a chemical compound
can wash away lifetimes of hurt
when alcohol only numbs
as it widens the wound

there can be healing
in what we hold in our hands.
in how we hold our two hands.
but we must loosen our fists first.

selective hearing

there are more cries for help
absorbed by the walls on this street
than there are ears willing to burden
themselves with the truth.

we are of homes that glisten
on the outside and combust
behind closed doors

repentant when it is too late.
silent when it is not.

i gave you my most
delicate thoughts
and they would seldom
land somewhere soft

no sharpened edges
in your chest ever melted
to fresh water like i told
myself they would

maybe this is where
my ice comes from.

someone once told me that pressure makes diamonds
what she
forgot to mention was that
although what they become can never be scratched, their
walls are so hardened that they will shatter whatever
they please, tough as the pressure that let them be
so maybe that's why my insides look so
much like a struggle that should
have set me
free

does water remember
when she is stilled into
silence
all the ways that she can
strangle and devour?

does she recall
when she is vengeful
all the ways that she can
pour life into the aching?

there are lives upon lives
crumbling and rising
within a being all at once.
you are more
always   more
than what fills your body
                    right now.

listen. a pen isn't a surgical instrument.
you can't reach inside and begin to dissect
as if what's within is meant to be held and
rearranged by the skill of your hand. as if
you won't encounter vein and nerve and
critical artery. as if all your probing will
only lead to her catharsis. when you scrape
her edges in the name of introspection, you
won't just hear buzzer—the electric shock
will course through her body even though
it may never reach yours. this ink isn't
operation. these infected wounds do not
make for masterful storytelling and you
never even asked for permission before
you began to open skin in the first place.
why hold this thing like a scalpel when,
if anything, it is a window?

lung (n)

one of the pair of respiratory organs seated within the rib cage. swallows what is needed and spreads it across the body. gathers what is not needed and releases it from the body. in a constant dance between fullness and emptiness. requires both states and every place in between to function. offers life through an elaborate array of branches. of roots. transports that which goes ignored until it is in short supply. shows me how to rise and fall and rise. and fall. frightens when separated from sustenance. when confined. demands to be freed when threatened with shackles. quivers. aches. screams. falls out of tune with itself until willed into steadiness.

what does it feel like?

like my lungs are caving in. like i can't breathe.

quiet tongue heavy head

i have often known
the heaviest hearts
to recite the lightest words
and the burdenless
do not understand
that to dive headfirst
into oceans like ours
is to surely drown

so we skim the surface
and fill pages to become empty
and tie up our stories carefully
and do not unravel
because minds like these
are not easily stitched back together
when torn at the seams.

think about it

i am told to stop
thinking so much

and i wonder why
it is that in order to
survive in this world
i must not use
my mind.

there is no way
to live in a body
on an earth
in a universe
this complex
and not carry
questions in
your pockets
like accumulated
change

i have come to fear
my lack of answers
far less than humans
who claim to have
them all.

morale-ity

my greatest fear is that we are nothing more
than a collection of bad guys and
for-the-greater-good guys. that we are all
colored in different shades of compromise.

that fear overrides truth.

that we deal ideals like decks of cards
abandoning the hands that no longer work
in our favor as easily as we lied when
we said we cared about each other.

what is this messy, muddy life
in which i can say everything except what i actually mean
    i can breathe but never catch my own breath
    i can be everyone that my words dance between
    but an unraveling, worn-out being

i can shatter
                                        only when the pieces fall like mosaic
they stand above
watch
marvel at the broken
gather up their inspiration
and walk away

the empowerment
that i seek does not
degrade other women

i will not suffocate
someone with that
which allows me
to breathe.

when i lost my center all these planets
fell out of orbit, mercury split himself
open on venus's skin. mars tried to
become his own source of stability.
earth & her moon somehow fell out of
love & my heart wandered quietly into
a dark, empty nothing.

i didn't die you know but i drifted

& drifted & drifted waiting for
inevitable collision or unyielding cold.
when i lost my center everything in my
sky fell up & down so i gravitated
toward the closest form of warmth.
there were no flames no lights no
loves. steady enough to put me back in sync.

you tell me that you are grateful that i am
here. that the world is better for my presence
that maybe things would have been different
if i never was that maybe my being has
helped another being be and

i am twenty-five years into this body.
pouring into the ink black of your eyes.
sitting atop a spherical classroom that my
people know to be alive. wondering how to
meet me knowing that i will leave me.
wondering how i found myself on this
tightrope where i must walk until i let go.
wondering what i am supposed to do with
love if i am only learning how to wash it
away. wondering how much longing exists
in all the spaces between space. wondering
if all the ache. all the separation between life
and death still hangs somewhere in the air
after centuries and centuries of all these
humans yearning for love and god and
themselves and each other. wondering if the
earth could even carry such a burden. almost
certain (but never certain) that sadness and
suffering and fear can only exist in minds of
the living. almost certain that somewhere,
between the fabric of oxygen, and
attachment, and all my questions. there is a
universe that is still. and still breathing. and
okay.

i've tried boarding up the windows
with deep breathing and changing
all the locks on my thoughts but
when anxiety moves into my body
i am pushed out onto the street
with nothing but a box of crushed
courage and a few flimsy distractions
to hold me over until she decides it is
time to leave.

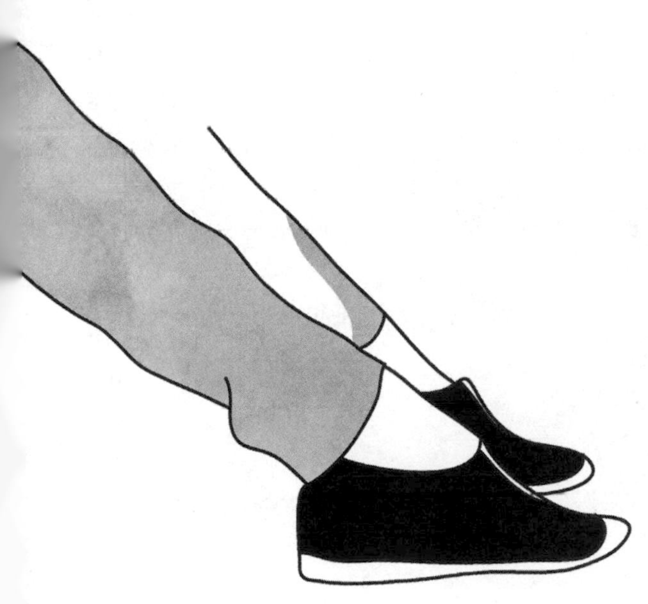

depression
is this ghost
that looms
over my
shoulder
& nobody
seems to
believe in
in spirits.

sometimes
my body feels like
nothing more than a metal conductor
for the emotions of others
& i open my chest not knowing
the weight i already carry

i want to hold you
i want to hold you
i want to hold you

but i haven't yet learned how to hold myself.

all this went down at once

level three, room nine, maternity

one woman breaks the silence at
this small being who is five hours
and seventeen minutes into a world
that refuses to need her: *look, at least*
her skin is fair. and a woman who is
five hours and seventeen minutes into
motherhood screams. allows fourteen
hours and thirty-two minutes of labor
and an epidural that didn't help to pour
through her vocal cords. demands that
they all leave if they cannot be awestruck
at this small being worthy of all the
space she takes up in this world. and
an ocean pours from her red-rimmed
eyes. and a nurse comes running. and a
small being wakes and raises her voice.
and a grandmother who refuses to be
awestruck by a miracle looks to her son
for support. his eyes show her the door.

level two, room fourteen, mental health

six people gather in a circle. a black-haired
woman crosses her legs with a book open in
her lap. two boys lock eyes. a lanky girl stares
absentminded out the window. a soft-eyed
person stretches their arms up to the ceiling

palms upturned in almost prayer. and you. you
are here without anyone else knowing. it's
freeing, isn't it? to be gone just this once. for
them to think you are at the top of a ski hill and
not here.
trying to climb up from the bottom of so many
different things. *how do you feel today*?
(like my lungs are not collapsing. like
everything is not a mistake. like i am not
a mistake. like i do not need to erase myself
to fix myself. like i am not a single branch
floating in an upset sea. like there is something
bright out there. that maybe. just maybe.
it is for me.)
today? i feel—i feel good.

level one, room twenty-nine, sacred space

she walks in between my sobs. begins to vacuum
the floor before she catches my eye before i can
shield my face before i can pretend i do not need
help. asks me what's wrong and is greeted
by my silence. asks me if it is because of someone
in the hospital and it is hollowing the way the
story comes so quickly. the patient that does
not exist and the surgery that does not exist
because i am better at building gates than
opening doors. the arms around my body
work, though. for a moment, someone
hears and this is enough.

it's not that i think
poems are meant
to be woven from
all the knots in my chest

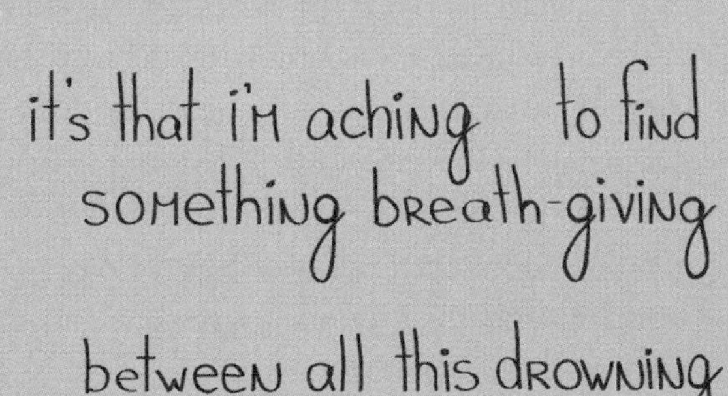

it's that i'm aching to find
something breath-giving

between all this drowning

a post on the internet insists that i am exactly where i need to be and i don't double-tap. partly because i am a cynic but mostly because i hate it when people promise me things that they are not entirely sure of. right now i am sprawled across my bed and do concede that i am quite content where i currently am but what if i was on a musty train slapped to someone's armpit or an empty road with an empty tank of gas or the edge of a rooftop on a far-too-tall building   i wonder if it is possible for things to happen in my generation just because they happen   and not because someone needs to sell a lesson   that offers the pinching satisfaction of a digital heart   if i survive but do not have a pretty story of triumph do i still have a body? if i find myself lost even after i write the poem about being found is there still light within me? if i fall into all this hurt and there is nothing beautiful to show for it, am i still here?   i wonder if it is possible for things to happen just because they happen   and yet i wonder if it is true. that things can get better. that my mind can will itself in a new direction. that i can go as far as i take myself.   i am cynical but i am also desperate.

the one he asked me to write about prison

i doubt you've heard doors bang shut as loud as the ones right beneath my chest. it's an echo chamber in here. where every breath and sigh and desperate shout to love seems like it can only call back to me. where i am heard by the only voice that has ever known me.

these walls. thick and soundproof. know how to sever me from my heart / cut away all feeling / slice away any sense of who i was / and tell me that they are holding me close.

closer than you ever did.

i convince myself that it is safe here. because the only one left within is the one who i can trust. the only one who will not leave when the heat of summer is fire upon the cement and winter wraps its breath around my neck. the only one who will not break through these locks to take all the pieces of me still in my possession.

do you remember the night i left all my tears on your skin? each one worth more than any prayer. tell me how you pushed them away without a second thought. tell me how you watched my skin turn to concrete without wrapping your arms around me. when i placed my heart in your hands only to watch it slip through your fingers, there were only questions left to grasp:

where did all those whispers go when i sent them to you? can you send them back to me? can you stand to look at me?

trilokpuri

there are gaping holes in my chest that i often forget about.
bullets labeled genocide lodged so deep that i've never
bothered pulling them out. the threshold for human pain
only extends so far but, truthfully, i fear the sight of the blood
more than anything else

huddled in the seat before me is a four-year-old with eyes
bluer than asphyxiation. eyes that see only good:
good people. good things.

the bus turns right onto clearbrook. left on blueridge as the
skies darken to a shade of char. lurch left again at trilokpuri

there is silence within this hearse as darkness approaches
ever faster in the form of flame   men with alcohol
poured in their eyes approach   their reasoning
systematically sedated

they do not see children or hear my mother's pleas.
they light our funeral pyre as this bus desperately begs to
escape on tires that have already been slashed and suddenly

i find myself wondering how darkness can consume minds
far faster than a pair of hands can reach around a throat.
how men can regard wombs as storage houses for knives.
how the light drawn out of the chests of my family members
could ever be called *casual*
how a war could be waging within my own body between
freedom and oppression for thirty-five years and i am still
too afraid to watch the bullets fall from my chest.

in the end, it is not the smoke that we all suffocate on
but the
silence

smoke can consume a pair of lungs but silence consumes
generations and as the smoke lifts upon punjab and the
flames subside it is the silence that remains
and i know no death more frightening.

and if my words do not find you well
if they find you curled up beneath
the covers with eyes that hurt to open
if they find you running out the back door
barefoot because the flip-flops will
only slow you down as you leave
if they find you pushed into a corner
both of room and mind, knee-deep
in all the people who you regret
i only hope that my words can sit
with you a while and hold you.
that you can rest your head on
their shoulders. that they help
you untangle all the mess
that other words have left.

if the words hold you hostage, both refusing to be spoken and refusing to let you leave. if the words feel like burden, no longer art but obligation. if the words are a cement cage, forcing you to move only in endless circles. if the words are an elaborate arrangement of plates but you are not hungry. if the words are a butcher's knife, cutting too deep into all the parts of you that are tender. if the words are a hollowed vessel of what was once a tree growing within you. if the words are expensive, but leave you empty when they are not draped across your neck. if the words are a red heart, a double tap, a closed fist with a raised thumb. if the words are a responsibility, a burden, a curse, a dying thing. if the words do not free you, why do you hold on to them?

she is listless when she comes
to me at 3:46 in the morning.
heart the foggy color of
exhaustion and eyes welling
with something honest that
he is too afraid to meet.

she asks
when do things
start getting better?

and i tell her that they don't
until better is demanded.
that we are products of struggle
and sometimes there is no way
to convince the heart that
this is beautiful.

i want to get better

but i'm in the habit
of scrubbing the walls
clean only to redecorate
identically.
of running for so long
i somehow end up
where i started.
of returning
to all the places
that hurt.

that night in the mountains
we talked about all the stars
we can't see from the city
and i thought about the few
that manage to break through
the pollution to make us
wonder about all the others

my loved ones say
there are galaxies twinkling
within me and i look up
into the night sky
searching for something
bright enough to make me
believe it.

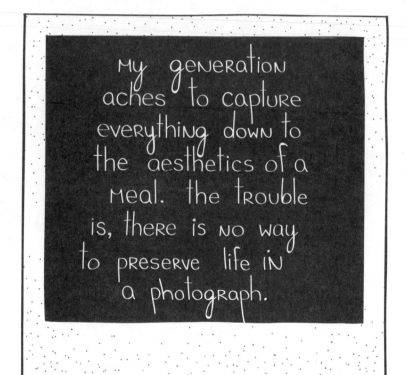

my generation aches to capture everything down to the aesthetics of a meal. the trouble is, there is no way to preserve life in a photograph.

if there was a way
to tear open the seams of time and space
to find you. if there was a way to reach into
the place where all the pain lived
and stitch it up forever
we would have. i would have.
with these two hands i would have.

for harsimran singh, 1998–∞

while a new year arrived somewhere in the world,
ice enveloped our entire city. not snow. ice. when
the freezing rain came and stayed, it looked something
like a glass village or whoville or a breathtakingly
cold dream

last night, more people than i can count offered their
shoulders as places to cry. their kindness was the only
thing that warmed me. when you left, you took all of us
with you and we inherited all the hurt

this morning, we awoke for the first time in a world without
your smile. the icicles began melting today, slipping from
the trees in chunks. in dripping water. all this earth wept
with us, too.

the loss makes hollowed fruit of me.
and i am emptied and scraped clean
of myself. but there are still seeds.
somewhere. in these blinking eyes
and expanding lungs.
and today, i will show myself
that these are signs of life.

i count all the prayers we would pool together
for the chance to ask you to stay
but then i reach for this word *love*
place it between my fingers and resist the urge
to crush it to powder hold it on my tongue
until i do not need to spit it out whisper it
to myself until it does not seem like the most
frightening thing i have ever felt
remember every you within me that has
wanted to go. sit softly with all the times that
we have lived.

if you see a human being
and do not see a human   being.
if you see a human being and only
see a body to walk over. their back
a bridge between here and where
you thirst to plant your feet. i will
not lie and claim you will never
get far but i am certain that you
will only get further from the
human   you used to be.

if you treat yourself like a poem
that needs to be read aloud
that requires hours of analysis
that contains a background story
behind each metaphor
and context beneath each word
how is it that you can dismiss others
as one-dimensional characters
static and stock
from the beginning to the end
of the story you have written
about them?

what good is it to be called a wildflower
when your own roots hold you hostage
i cannot exist here anymore
where i am forced to sit still
while my skin is trampled upon by strangers

if the wind caught me   & took me with her
i would be promised no safety but at least
i would not be stagnant.

the inextricable feeling while i am waiting
for this plane to arrive that i am supposed
to be boarding a different one. that there is
somewhere else waiting for me—wherever
the hell *else* is. that i am only moving further
away. that closer is at another terminal.

nerve (n)

filamentous bands of tissue that conduct impulses across the entire body. use electricity to spark reactions. reasoning. choices. an elaborate garden of feeling. the reason why we do what we do. think what we think. know what we know. or don't know. brings the whole city of your skin alive with their touch. raises each hair to attention and showers you with goose bumps. allows you to shiver at their sight and feel your heart race. feel your lungs expand. feel your muscles tense up and relax. feel light wash over you. cut off from its network, it can shut off the streetlights in an entire neighborhood. sometimes for a season. sometimes for a lifetime.

nerves are underrated.

i don't think we notice them
until they're gone.

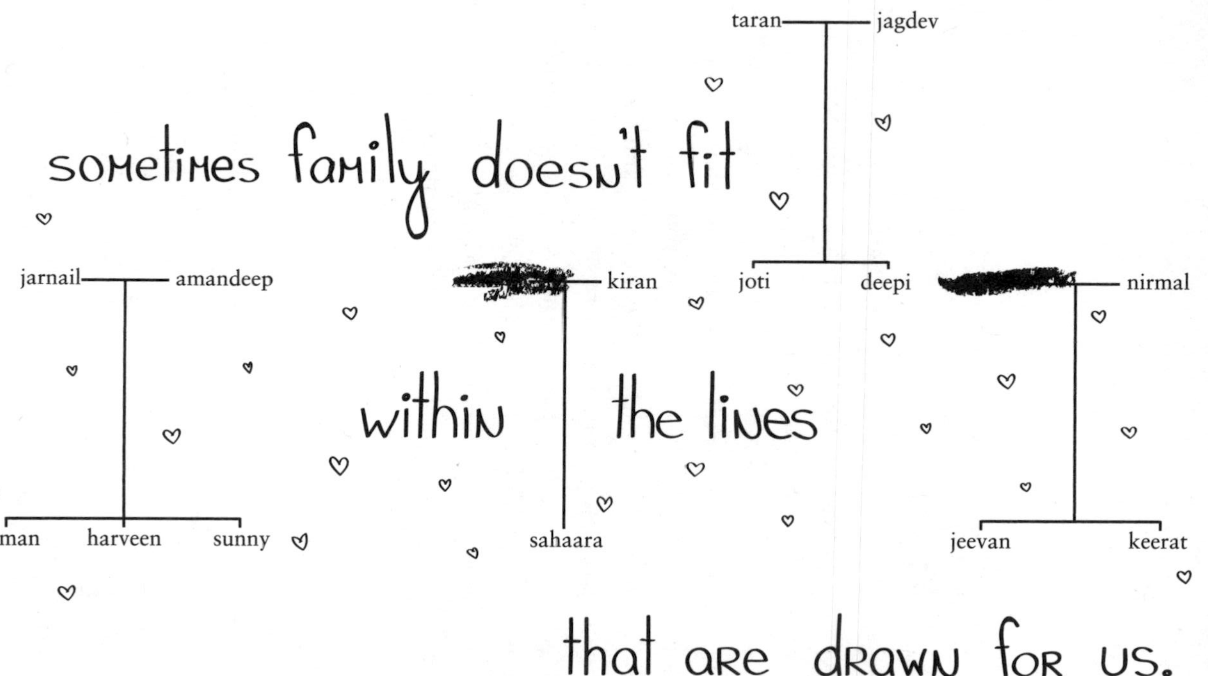

sometimes family doesn't fit

within the lines

that are drawn for us.

kiran

august 17, 2001

There is something about flight that has always brought me close to hope. At that moment when the wheels of a plane slip away from the earth, I am reminded that I have just defied gravity. I am no longer anchored to where I came from, no longer bound there by science or geography or coincidence. By heart? That is, perhaps, another matter. Nevertheless, in this fraction of time between two different worlds, there is a chance to rewrite my story.

"So why are you traveling?" His question was sudden and unexpected. Ten hours of silence and I had thought I could get away with four more. No such luck.

My eyes were transfixed on the clouds that swallowed the sky. He was almost as surprised as I was when the words escaped my mouth: "I'm running away."

My sight remained glued to the clouds, but I could feel his almond eyes watching me. As the cloud cover gave way momentarily, I caught a glimpse of tiny fields below. I tried to let their smallness sink in.

Small. Everything is small. Just like your problems.

Just like him. Or her.

He was still staring at me. Just as my lips began to form the shape of words my mother would probably tell me to never speak aloud, he responded. "We're all running away from something. Seven thousand miles is pretty far to be running, though. Do you think you've really thought this out?" The corner of his mouth was turned up in a smirk. A part of me wanted to tear it from his face. I wasn't sure what his intentions were, but I couldn't recall having solicited the advice of a stranger.

"Maybe I don't have any other options," I replied with well-trained coolness. It was the coolness that I used for years at the dinner table with my father. It was a well-rehearsed charade for both of us. Dad pretended to be interested and I pretended to be honest.

"We all have options," he said, slipping his copy of the *Business Times* into the seat compartment before him. "Pretty girl like you, dressed like that—I'm inclined to think you have options."

For the first time I let my eyes lock onto his. I said each word slowly and deliberately, hoping that his reply would die in his throat: "Screw off. You don't know me."

"Well . . . what are you running from, then?" he asked, eyes still trying to decode mine. His gaze held for a fraction too long, as though he was not simply curious but hungry.

"Gangsters," I replied with the most stoic expression I could muster. "My father is a drug lord who controls half of the Punjab-Pakistan border. Our mansion in Chandigarh was built on drug money. But drugs are a rise-and-fall sort of game, you know? We've got enemies all over the place. I doubt as far as Canada, though." I stretched out my arm in a rather dramatic attempt to examine my nails and then looked to gauge his reaction. He was unimpressed.

"Fine. You don't have to tell me. Keep your mask on." He laughed, scratching his boardroom-smooth cheek.

"I don't wear a mask."

"Okay."

For a while, we returned to silence. A world spun ceaselessly inside my head and I wondered what orbited within his. It occurred to me, at some point, that each and every person sitting in this plane contained a world of their own—their own fears, their own joys, their own burdens to bear. Yet here we all were, a thousand miles above all the problems that we were running from. A thousand miles above all the collisions that were yet to be. I love the way a plane makes your world seem so small, the way it makes everything seem so distant. The trouble with planes, however, is that they land, and when they land, you can't hide anymore.

I watched as the sun slowly handed the sky over to the moon. Know-it-all to my right dozed off, which I was grateful for. I doubted that he'd say anything more for the rest of the flight, though.

I was wrong. When we finally landed, he got up to grab his carry-on and handed me mine as well.

"You know you can say thank you, right?" he scoffed.

"I didn't ask for help."

"Maybe you should," he offered me one last inquisitive look and turned away just before tears began to well up in my eyes.

Help was the one thing that I was certain I could not ask for.

kiran

august 18, 2001

When I landed, the earth did not immediately shatter. This was unexpected. The normalness of my uncle's hug and my aunt's casual conversation and the rainy drive away from the airport dizzied me.

"How's your mom doing?" my aunt asked.

My hands, delicately stacked one upon the other, tensed ever so slightly.

"She's good, Chachi Jee. She's not working anymore but she still designs suits," I replied.

"Oh yeah? Where's my suit, then?" She laughed effortlessly. Her laughter was always surprising. It is the day to my mother's night. My mother's laughter is seldom so carefree.

"That," I said smilingly, "you'll find out when we get home."

She looked back with kind eyes that said, *You shouldn't have*. My mom's eyes can speak like that, too.

The intensity of my mother's gaze at the New Delhi airport was still floating in my mind. Just after I handed my oversize suitcases to the sugar-polite airline attendant, I looked back at Mom and Dad. Mom's features were arranged in the way I had expected. She spoke to me wordlessly: *Go to school. Finish well. Come back and everything will be fine.*

All right.

I tried to interest myself in the sights outside the window: cement and tall buildings and soon the endless expanse of a freeway. Breathe in. Breathe out. I steadied myself with the way the moon followed us faithfully no matter how fast the car traveled. It was the same moon, ivory and luminescent, that I stared up at from my bedroom back in Chandigarh. Guess I hadn't traveled halfway across the world all alone, after all.

The lights gently illuminated the streets when we finally got home. The time difference between Punjab and Vancouver had me wide awake, despite the lateness of the night. The cold Canadian air, which would feel like a surprise for months, wrapped its arms around me as I stepped out of the car. So this was home.

My uncle fumbled with his keys in the darkness as he opened the trunk.

"Don't worry, Kiran, I've got it," he said as I attempted to help him with my luggage. "You and your chachi go inside."

My uncle's home looked nothing like our gated house back in Chandigarh. My father's rising position within the car company meant that he was able to cross off half of his travel list by the age of forty-five: Barcelona, Dubai, Tokyo, and Paris. For whatever reason, however, cities in North America were never very high on his list. It was only with my grandmother's insistence that my parents had decided to visit my aunt and uncle in Canada. At the time, I was eight and my aunt and uncle lived in a tiny apartment in Surrey. The little home was constantly buzzing with sound, mostly that of Joban, my baby cousin. As a young girl, I couldn't put a finger on what it was, but something about that house felt different from my own. There was a warmth there that had nothing to do with weather.

Eleven years later, I was back. This time, on my own. This

time, no longer the child assured of her place between her mother and father. This time, standing on unsteady legs that would have no one to guide them. It was everything that I needed and everything I dreaded.

My aunt and uncle lead me up to the bedroom closest to the stairway.

"I'll go wake up Joban," Chachi Jee said. "He'll want to see you."

"No, no. Let him sleep. I'm actually really tired, too," I replied.

"Okay, you should get some rest. But call your parents first and let them know you've arrived."

"Okay," I whispered.

It had been approximately seventeen hours since I had decided that the first time I called her, I would tell her the truth.

"Only a few years of school and then we have the wedding! I talked to Prabh's mom the other day. I swear that woman must have everything her way. She knows this new designer from Bangladesh—Mukherjee something—and she insists that he—"

"Mom?" I paused, absorbing the momentary silence between my end of the receiver and hers, a distant world away.

"Hanji," she replied, her voice, so familiar and unbending.

"I'm pregnant."

I let the words settle into the space between us. I didn't breathe.

"What do you mean?"

"I mean . . . I'm pregnant."

"This is why I told you to be careful when you are alone with him! It doesn't matter whether you are engaged or not. A man is still a man."

I hesitated for a moment. I couldn't bring myself to tell her.

"You stupid girl."

The receiver remained to my ear and I found myself sliding to the ground, pulling my knees up to my chin. The wood floor beneath me was cold against my naked feet. At once, I was in Chandigarh again, two days before I had boarded the plane. The waterfall at the Rock Garden bloomed before me, its rushing waters juxtaposed with the tears streaming down my face. Prabh finally spoke. His almost jet-black eyes piercing into mine for the first time.

"And I'm supposed to believe you over my own brother?" he hissed in a frigid whisper.

"Why—*why*—would I lie about something like this?!" I angrily retorted.

He stared at me with something cold and foreign shadowing his features. Something indifferent in place of the loving outrage I had expected. How could I have been so stupid?

The silence on the phone was the length of either a moment or a lifetime. I had almost willed myself to say something when she finally spoke up.

"Is the abortion already scheduled? You should already have medical covera—"

"Mom, I'm . . . keeping this child."

"And how do you think I'm supposed to plan a wedding, your wedding, before it starts to show that you are pregnant? You have the rest of your bloody life to have children with him."

Then came the part that was somehow just as overwhelming. The words slipped from my lips before I could even stop myself.

"I'm not going to marry him, either." With that, I ended the call.

kiran

i don't think there was ever a way
for me to be the right type of immigrant
i remember the day at the grocery store

when i told that man there was no discount
on milk and he slammed the jug on the counter
and called me a useless paki bitch
like the least i could do for living on his land
was honor an expired coupon.

and he didn't know me. and my accent was much
softer than gurjeet's. and i never rolled my r's.
and i never wore my salwar kameez in public

but my skin was a siren
that was always too loud.

kiran

march 3, 2002

When I realized that I had a choice, it momentarily felt like light. Despite every consequence of this decision, the small being blossoming within my body could be mine. And it wasn't just the fact that I could choose to keep the baby. It was the fact that I could make a decision altogether. About my own life. About my own womb. Having a choice felt as new to me as morning sickness in the first trimester: it was foreign and overwhelming. I couldn't imagine that something like this would ever feel the same for another woman, but in the face of an entire lifetime that felt outside of my control, this choice somehow made me feel as if my body could belong to me.

I don't think I ever really had an option when my parents asked me if I wanted to go to school in Canada after rattling off every reason why a good education was important in marrying into a good family. When my dad told me that biology was the ideal path to take in university. When I was introduced to Prabh. My parents, open-minded in their own eyes, never thought of it as anything close to an arranged marriage, but I think we could both feel the expectation after our first date.

"So what do you think of him?" said Mom, eyes wide with interest as soon as Prabh left our house. He had stepped inside to chat with my mom because it would have been disrespectful to just drop me off at the front door.

"I mean—he was nice. I want to get to know him better," I replied, still figuring out what exactly I felt.

"Good, good. There will be more time to get to know him. There doesn't need to be an announcement or an engagement very soon."

I remember the way my stomach flipped at the thought of her seeing so far into us after that first lunch we ate alone. Sometimes it felt like she only saw me in the distance and never in the present. I doubt she would be able to see how all of this hurt. I was the child who would have to live up to her in-laws' expectations. Her husband's expectations. Her expectations. Her second-place trophy in the face of a family that had expected a son. Her daughter who would have to fulfill their collective dreams in other ways. I don't think she could have seen any of this coming. Neither could I.

I was drawn back to the hospital room when Joti squeezed my hand. She was practically leaning out of her chair with a smile that spilled into her honey-brown eyes.

"How are you feeling, sweetie?" she asked.

"The contractions are getting worse. God—it feels like someone's kneading my stomach with a knife. And my back," I managed. I tried to tell myself that this pain was here for a reason. That it was my body's way of telling me that Sahaara was ready for this world. That we were in a painful dance with one another. That she was preparing to meet me. The throbbing hurt washed away all my thoughts, though. Every time a contraction came, I had to erase the contents of my mind and ride through the waves of pain until they let me go.

"Hang in there . . . they're going to do the epidural soon, okay?" Somehow, Joti's words felt like a reassuring promise. I knew she was trying her best to fill every empty chair in this hospital room. With her septum piercing and boyish haircut,

Joti was the type of woman who would have made my mom's eyes fall out of her head. The thought of her daughter ever befriending such a person would have been laughable.

"Thank you," I whispered.

"For what?"

"For being here. For literally everything," I replied, struggling to look her in the face with tears in my eyes. I'd never been good at sharing my softness, but this last year had only made it infinitely harder. Every bitter-cold moment became another brick in the wall, Joti's kindness the only force warm enough to break through.

"Listen. Stop. This is what family is for," she said with as much seriousness as she could muster beneath a tearful smile. Her eyes glistened beneath the dim lighting and the silent spaces between us were filled with soft acoustic music. The calming CD had been her idea. As she wiped her eyes, Dr. Shirazi walked in, holding a chart with one hand and adjusting her mauve hijab with the other.

"How are you doing, Kiran?" she said, a gentle smile deepening her dimples. Just like Joti's presence was an immense relief, I felt utterly grateful for Dr. Shirazi. Her compassion felt just as consistent today as it had the day I first met her, when she seemed to understand the things I couldn't tell her. She saw the way I was shaking when she was getting ready to examine me that day and asked if she could hold my hand. I somehow think she knew what happened. How I'd gotten pregnant. That night began to resurface in my mind. I tried to push the nightmare away before it engulfed me.

"I'm okay. Are we doing the epidural now?"

"Yes, very soon. I'd just like to see how dilated you are first? Is it okay if I check your cervix?" she said, her voice always upturned at the ends of her sentences as if she were asking a question. She sat down between my legs and measured to see how close I was to ten centimeters, which was when I could start pushing. I swear, I had to be at ten centimeters by now.

"So we're still at four," she said, looking up from her wide-framed glasses. "We're just going to have to keep waiting. But we're going to get you that epidural now, okay? The anesthesiologist is on her way."

I let out an audible sigh. I had known it was going to be bad. Everyone said the pain was unbearable. But it was one thing to hear someone talk about it and another to feel a contraction run its ugly way through my abdomen. No description could have prepared me for it.

"Sorry it took me a few minutes—I was tied up with another patient," came the breathless voice of a tiny, blond-haired woman who had just walked in. "Hi, I'm Dr. Morrison. I'll be doing your epidural today."

I nodded and attempted a smile.

"I'm going to incline your bed a bit and then get you to sit up."

I slowly sat up, and she turned her back to me as she prepared the needle.

"So what's going to happen is . . . I'm going to numb your lower back with a bit of local anesthetic. Then the needle for the epidural is going to go into your back. I'm going to need you to arch your back and try to stay as still as you can while it goes in"—she turned toward me and nodded kindly—"and then we're going to have the catheter go in—"

"Sorry—what's a catheter?" I asked, still learning my way around some English terms.

"Oh, yes—a catheter is just a small tube. And that's where the epidural medication will come from. We'll tape it down to your back so it stays in place," she patiently told me. Her thorough explanation helped me feel a bit more calm.

"There are some risks associated with the epidural. You may experience a spinal headache, loss of bladder control. In uncommon situations, there may be temporary nerve damage that will disappear in a few days or weeks, but sometimes months. There is also a risk of infection and permanent nerve damage," Dr. Morrison rattled off as my eyes widened. "And I know those risks sound scary but serious complications with an epidural are rare and millions of women receive epidurals without a problem. Would you like to go ahead with the procedure?"

"Um . . . yeah . . . I don't know how I'm going to do this otherwise."

As Dr. Morrison wiped my back with antiseptic and inserted the local anesthetic just as she described, she said, "Now, you might feel some pain as the needle goes in. I'm going to need you to try to stay as still as you can. Go ahead and take a big, deep breath."

I held Joti's hand tight as sharp pain coursed in my lower back.

"All right, we're going to do the epidural now. You shouldn't feel a thing," said Dr. Morrison.

"So are you two sisters?" a nurse in pink scrubs asked as she assisted Dr. Morrison with needles and tubes.

"No . . . Joti's a friend," I replied.

"Ah . . . you look like sisters, though," she said as we looked each other up and down and stifled laughter. We looked absolutely nothing alike. We both just happened to be brown.

"So your family—are they on their way right now? They must be so excited!" the nurse asked with a well-meaning smile.

"Janine—" Dr. Shirazi began.

"Kiran's family is back home in Punjab. They won't be able to make it for the birth," interrupted Joti. Something about her tone caused Nurse Janine to smile and say nothing more. I tried to just focus on breathing.

"You're doing great, Kiran!" Dr. Shirazi chimed encouragingly. "It's going to take between ten to thirty minutes for the epidural to kick in, so we're going to have to try our best to be patient for it?"

I nodded, as Joti helped me ease my way back down onto the bed. I stared up at the gray ceiling, at the fetal heart monitor that recorded my baby's steady heartbeat. My hands clenched the bed as another contraction violently squeezed my abdomen and I wondered when this was all going to end.

The epidural took its sweet time, but once it arrived, the contraction pain melted away. I could still feel all the pressure of my baby bearing down on me as she made her very slow arrival into this world, but most of the throbbing aches had departed. All the anxiety, however, still pulsated through me. What would it feel like when I held her in my arms for the first time? Would it be like what Joti's mom described—overwhelmingly beautiful? What if all those motherly instincts that Aunty Jee talked about didn't kick in? What if I wasn't ready for this?

"Tell me about her name," said Joti, sensing all the tension on my face and hoping to keep me distracted. "Why Sahaara?"

"Well . . . it means 'support ' in Punjabi. 'Shelter.' 'Refuge.' I guess I just . . . I want to be her refuge. I want to keep her safe. Because I wasn't. Does that make sense?"

"It does," Joti murmured, going quiet for a few moments. "Thank you for sharing that with me."

Dr. Shirazi stepped in again to check in on me. It had been eight hours since the epidural and I was getting used to the idea that we were going to be here for a lot longer than I had originally anticipated.

"Wow, your cervix has gone from six to eight centimeters in the last hour. Looks like baby is on her way."

"Holy shit," I gasped. "This is happening."

Joti's eyes were wide. "This is happening."

After all that waiting, it felt like ten centimeters came way sooner than I was prepared for. But, I mean, it could have been ten hours later and would I have been any more ready? If everything went as planned, I was about to be a mom. . . .

And where was my mom? Another thought that I needed to push away.

The concept of childbirth had always scared the hell out of me. As in, where in this tiny frame was a baby supposed to fit? How was it supposed to come out of me? And yet, this was happening. This baby was making her way through me and I was doing what felt like the impossible. I was trying my best to breathe just like Dr. Shirazi and Joti had been coaching me to. Trying to focus all my energy on pushing the right way. But I wasn't prepared for the flashback—the memory that tore into my skin as Sahaara tried to make her way out. The body that had entered mine nine months earlier when I had done everything in my power to scream the word *no*. I didn't realize that the bloodcurdling scream I heard in this hospital room was my own until Joti squeezed my hand tighter and placed her other hand on my head.

"We're almost there, love. We can do this, okay?" came Dr. Shirazi's steady voice. "One more big push and then we can take a break?" I could feel the blood rushing to my face as I focused all my remaining energy into this push.

"I can't do it anymore. I'm too—I'm too tired. I can't do this. I can't—" I cried.

"I know, love. You've done amazing! We've got her head out. I want you to just breathe and rest right now, okay?" I took a deep breath in and exhaled. I'd never felt so tired in my life.

"All right, we're going to go back underwater, okay? I need you to take a big breath and . . . push. Ten seconds. One . . . two . . . three . . . four . . . five . . . six . . . seven—you're doing amazing—nine . . . and ten. And let's go again. Almost there. One . . . two . . . three . . ."

I couldn't hear her anymore. All I knew was that I needed this baby out of me. I let out a messy shriek without any embarrassment—just as messy as this white bed had become. I didn't care who was listening. I just needed this shit to be over.

"One more big push, Kiran! And . . . you did it! She's here."

I shut my eyes and felt my hands shaking. Suddenly, there was a small body pressed against mine, covered in blood and all sorts of fluid. When they placed her on my chest and she began to cry, something swelled within me. The past twelve hours or fifteen hours or God knows how long disappeared. The entire world melted away. All the pressure in my body somehow evaporated to nothing. Perhaps there were problems somewhere out there, people dealing with their own stresses and pain, but in this moment nothing existed but this love. This sudden and all-consuming force that had seemingly come out of my body along with her. It was as if this beautiful, blinking, breathing being had never not been right here against my skin. It was as if I were floating. Tomorrow would come and we'd figure it out when we had to. Right now, however, there was only light.

sahaara

january 29, 2020

“And please make sure you say ‘here’ nice and loud when I call your—your name.” Ms. Harrison stumbles over her words when he knocks on the door. He catches my eye and grins while I do my best to stifle laughter. I can’t believe he’s actually trying to switch into this class. “Savreen, could you get the door, please?”

Sunny walks in with all of his usual nonchalance and goes straight to the teacher. He’s wearing dark jeans and the black bomber jacket that I admitted to liking during winter break.

“I didn’t realize Surrey jacks know how to write poems,” Sonam whispers to Harmeet. Before I can stop myself, I turn around and glare.

“Since when is he a jack?” I snap, despite myself. I'm sick of stupid terms like *Surrey jack* that place people in boxes.

“I mean . . . he doesn’t dress like a jack, but he definitely fights like one.”

I shake my head as I turn away from them. I can’t remember the last time I saw Sunny anywhere near a fight, but he has a reputation that follows him like a shadow. He’d die laughing if I ever shared something so corny, but sometimes I wish that people could see his light.

“Yeah . . . I wanted to switch into creative writing,” he says, passing Ms. Harrison a note.

She serves him a “teacher look” as she says, “I’m sorry. Monday was the last day to switch classes. I’m not accepting any more students.” She doesn’t look at the note.

“But Mr. Brar said I could switch in. He wrote me a note.

I really wanted to get into this class," he murmurs, just loud enough for me to hear from the middle of the room. She lets out an audible sigh and furrows her brow as she reads the message that Sunny somehow managed to extract from the school counselor.

"All right, well, Sundeep, please take a seat—"

"It's Sunny," he interrupts.

"I'm sorry?"

"I go by Sunny."

She raises her eyebrows, clearly irritated. Sunny takes this as his cue to sit down. He finds the seat to my left that I was forced to save for him.

Ms. Harrison begins attendance, going down a student list that is mostly populated by girls. With the addition of Sunny, there are now three guys in this class. I've never understood guys who are horrified by the idea of expressing themselves. To be honest, though, Sunny has never struck me as a poet. This should be interesting.

"I can't wait to cry about all my feelings," he whispers.

"You do realize that poetry's not just about crying, right? But I do reserve the right to read all your teary-ass poems."

"Not a chance." He smirks. "You can read my shit when the book comes out."

"Sahaara Kaur?" comes the teacher's voice. She pronounces it as "suh-hair-uh" and it irritates the hell out of me. It would be too awkward to correct her now, though.

"Here."

"Suh-hair-uh Kaur," Sunny whispers in his most Caucasian teacher accent, "what are you doing after school?"

"Why do you ask, *Sundeep*?" I retort, Punjabi accent dripping all over the name his parents gave him.

He puts his hand on his chest as he feigns shock at my invocation of "the name." "Well . . . I was wondering if you wanted to chill. We could go grab pizza or something."

"Not today . . . I have plans with Jeevan. Got a group project for science that we have to start."

"When's it due?"

I hesitate. "In two weeks."

He raises his eyebrows. "Yeah. You guys can work on it later. Ask Jeevan if he's cool with that." The nerve of this boy.

"Excuse me?" comes Ms. Harrison's raised voice, snapping us out of our conversation. "Sunny, was it? I'm not sure why you switched into my class if you only came here to distract my students."

"Oh, um, sorry." He straightens in his seat and stifles that stupidly cute smirk.

"You're welcome to switch into a gym class if that's a better place for you." At this, my eyes widen. What was that supposed to mean?

Sunny lowers his eyes and clenches his jaw. He doesn't say anything.

"So, as I was saying, I'm going to explain the homework assignment first and then we'll get into today's in-class activity. This week, I want you to reflect on your future. I actually want you to close your eyes right now and just pause to take this in."

I catch Sunny's eye and then follow her instructions.

"I want you to imagine yourself ten years into the future." She pauses and asks each question slowly. "What do you look like? What are you wearing? What are you passionate about? Where are you on your career path?"

I try to focus on her questions but anger simmers at the edges of my thoughts.

"Have you achieved your goals?"

Yeah, Sunny was talking, but so was I. Why was Sunny the only one who got yelled at?

"Where are you as you imagine yourself? Who is standing by your side?"

I imagine myself at the age of twenty-seven standing in an art gallery. The walls are lined with my paintings, and my cylindrical poetry installation stands gracefully at the center of the room. My mom is there, smiling at her own portrait with nothing but carefree joy caressing her face. I turn the corner and enter my art studio where I help my students discover their inner Kandinskys and Picassos. I would want each of them to feel at home in my classroom. Especially the ones who are taught that they don't belong. Sunny's clenched jaw blooms within my mind. So do my mom's weather-worn eyes.

I'm standing at the front steps amid the crowd of people rushing out away from school when I feel a hand on my shoulder.

"You're definitely busy today, huh?" Sunny asks.

"Yep. Let's do something later this week," I reply.

Sunny's friend Ryan emerges from the sea of students that surround us.

"You coming to Strawberry Hill?" Ryan asks, out of breath.

"No . . .why?"

"Sim and Gary are gonna scrap today."

Sunny shrugs. "Um . . . nah. I've got better things to do than watch random people fight."

Ryan laughs. "Yeah, I'm sure you do, thuglife."

"What's that supposed to mean?"

"Nothing, bro. I just heard you're selling weed now. Are you gonna hook me up?"

At this, I'm completely thrown off. I think it's apparent from my face because Sunny is looking at me with a mixture of worry and fear in his eyes. We're both silent. Sensing the tension, Ryan eyes us both and mumbles something about basketball before walking away.

"Sunny . . . he's just talking shit, right? You're not . . . are you?"

"It's . . . it's complicated, Sahaara. Can we just . . . can we talk about this later?"

I shake my head. "Right. Later."

Sahaara Kaur
January 30, 2020
Creative Writing 12

Prompt: Where do you see yourself in ten years?

ten years from now   i will grow into my body
this sun-drenched skin will belong to me
even though i was told i don't belong here

this phulkari will hang off my shoulder on stages
in galleries   in every space that welcomes me
without worry about the culture that cradles me

these hands will grasp my loved ones without
                              fear of being pulled away
because they didn't seek safety the right way

this country will realize that colonization can't
make it matter more than every indigenous
community that has held the earth
                              intimately and infinitely

this land will finally want my mother
this air will finally embrace my beloveds
and home will finally pronounce my name

Sunny Sahota
February 5, 2020
Creative Writing 12

Prompt: Where do you see yourself in ten years?
do you even see me present   right here   right now

the principal sees me as the brown boy
who does what brown boys are good for
my coach sees me as the kid who can't commit
to anything bigger than himself
my teachers see me as the one who won't go
any further than our neighborhood
my friends see me as the guy who's
always down to fight their battles
my enemies see me as a body missing bullet holes
the cops see me as yellow tape and paperwork
and a statistic ready for the list
my mom sees me as the son who will only break her heart
my dad sees me as a shattered dream he held
when i was small enough to be rocked in his arms
i see me as all the darkness that hangs above and below and inside me. a tangled web i wove and got caught in. a concrete wall between my conscience and my actions and everything else. a hardening heart that scares me more than i'd ever admit to any of them.

and i think   she sees me.

sunny

i'll never be able to tell them
that i'm just tired
of the way my dad
    cries when he thinks
    no one is listening

how the urgent pile of letters
constantly rises higher
a race against
flooding water

    how he misses an earth
    that didn't want to push him away
    the early-morning peace he felt
    nurturing an endless sugarcane field
    before the soil ran red
    before gunfire came looking
    for their heads and he knew
    he couldn't stay.

sahaara

august 31, 2020

"So this is it, hey?" he murmurs.

"What?" I reply, "Jeevan, I'm going to school. I'm not dying."

"You know what I mean." He sighs and reaches over to grab my sketchbook. I can't remember when we started doing this. Coming to places like Whytecliff as though we belong here, I mean. I try to push away the thought of the white couple that glared at us in the parking lot. The ebbing pattern of ocean water against the rocks keeps me at ease. I like to pick out patterns when I'm anxious. A steady wind rustles through the fir trees and I watch as something like a hawk soars away from its perch. It lands in a fir tree at the opposite end of us. There's something balanced about this place.

I trace my fingers over the grooves of the rock below me. I don't know who owns the earth, but the question has been eating at me lately. In social studies last year, Lorraine Bishop laughed when I suggested that Diwali should be a national holiday. Then she got angry.

"Maybe you should remember who started this country."

I wanted to remind her that it was not so long ago that Europeans landed here. I wanted to remind her that colonization had helped them amass a great deal of their wealth. I wanted to tell her about the Sto:lo, the Musqueam, the Kwantlen, all the peoples who lived deliberately on the earth in ways most would never bother to comprehend. Instead, I remained silent.

I hate how I do that.

I lean over and flip to the most recent page. He nods as though reading something profound.

"I like it," he says, "the phulkari looks dope." He glides his thumb over the intricate Punjabi clothing pattern running across the somber woman's body and flips the page to see more of my artwork: the reason why this scholarship was possible in the first place. He takes off his glasses and tries wiping them clean on his hoodie.

For a while, we're both silent. The rocky wall encircling this little opening in the forest is weathered and worn. I wonder if the earth ever exhausts of us humans.

"We always knew you were gonna go far, man. I just didn't think all of this was gonna happen so soon." His eyes are tired. They've been that way for a long time.

"I don't get it." I laugh. "I'm not leaving Surrey. I'm not even leaving home."

"It's just gonna be weird not seeing you at school every day."

"I know. But trust me, you'll live." I smirk as he rolls his eyes at me.

I change the subject. "How's your mom?" I ask.

"She's okay, I think. Better than before. Keerat and I have been trying not to think about my dad's release date . . . I don't know with my mom, to be honest. Some days, I can tell that she's happier and other days it's like she feels guilty that he's in prison or something." He is simultaneously young and old, just like me. It's probably why we're friends.

"How about your mom?" he asks.

"I mean . . . as good as she's going to be. I'm just trying to process everything, I guess. I still don't even understand how this is real life," I respond, eyes caught on the dimming sight of distant waves.

"There's gotta be human rights reasons why she can stay. Permanently. I mean . . . they can't make her leave, Jeevan. Right?" I feel the tears welling up.

"We're gonna figure this out, okay? We'll figure this out together." Jeevan wraps his arm around me.

The fears I had been working so hard to push to the back of my mind suddenly rush to the surface. *What if something happens while I'm gone at school? What if my mom needs help? What if she needs me?* I try to swallow all the guilt.

I pull my cell phone out from my purse. 7:52 p.m. I ease myself up from the rock with all the grace one can muster on dangerously uneven ground.

"We should get going," I whisper. He nods and leads the way.

Silent drives have never been uncomfortable, but tonight there is something hanging in the space between us. *Uncomfortable* isn't the right word, though. It's just a little heavy. I turn up the volume of the Dead Prez track playing. It works: my eyes stay open. Last night was another sleepless night. The sleeplessness is something that I've been learning to deal with. Along with the anxiety. There are always butterflies in my stomach. They have teeth and they like to remind me of it. As long as I stick to my breathing exercises, though, I'm usually fine.

When I get to Jeevan's house, he stays seated, as though lost in thought.

My phone lights up with a number that I recognize even though I deleted his name months ago.

(604) 339-1111: Hey

"Uh . . . Sunny just texted me," I whisper. Even within the darkness, I think I catch a trace of red across his cheeks.

"You serious? Are you gonna tell him off?" he asks.

I hesitate for a moment, and he shakes his head with an absentminded laugh.

Sahaara: I'm sorry...do I know you?

(604) 339-1111: Wow...deleted my number, huh? :/

Sahaara: What do you want?

(604) 339-1111: Chill man. Was just thinking about you. How you been?

I stare down at my phone, shocked at his nerve. How does he even have the balls to text me after everything that happened? Then, naturally, I do exactly what I shouldn't do.

Sahaara: I've been okay.

Sahaara: You?

(604) 339-1111: Same tbh. Would be nice to see you some time.

(604) 339-1111: Just saying. Pls don't kill me.

Sahaara: Lol that's probably not the best idea. For very obvious reasons.

(604) 339-1111: Probably not. But aren't those types of ideas usually the funnest?

"Is 'funnest' a word?" I say aloud.

Jeevan's head is resting on the window almost contemplatively. "Why are you responding? You need to look out for yourself, man."

(604) 339-1111: Anyways...if you decide you don't hate me, hmu. We can go to Boston Pizza like old times lol

"I know. You're right. It's just trippy how he turns up out of the blue." I think back to the day he switched into my creative writing class and try to push the thought of his grin out of my head. I save his number in my phone despite myself. Jeevan's phone starts to vibrate.

"And that's my mom calling me. Again. I'm gonna go inside before I get killed." Jeevan leans over to hug me and opens the door. Before he disappears through the door to his basement, he turns back to smile. He'll stop stressing eventually. Maybe I will, too.

I pull away from the curb and turn the corner. It isn't a coincidence that Jeevan lives a street away from me. I was ten when he moved into the neighborhood, his yard sharing its back fence with mine. I still remember seeing a miniature Jeevan, complete with his thick-framed glasses and Batman graphic T-shirt, attempting to haul a box through the back door of his house, only to have everything avalanche through the bottom. I saw the scene unfold as I peered through a circular hole in our wooden fence that afternoon. I attempted to stifle a laugh, as noise would spoil my espionage. Soon enough, however, I felt the need to weigh in on the situation.

"You know you're way too skinny to carry all that, right?" I chimed, propping myself up to the top of the fence with my elbows.

Jeevan stumbled and turned around in search of my voice. When he spotted me, his cheeks went plainly red, despite his walnut-brown skin.

"Yeah . . . well . . . you should mind your own business," he snapped back, a little lamp in one hand and a stack of comic books in the other.

"And you should do something less nerdy than collect comic books."

His cheeks flushed red again and he opened his mouth to say something, only to clench his jaw and gather up another pile of his belongings.

"My name is Sahaara."

"Whatever," he said as he slammed the door behind him.

"Whatever," I mumbled in response as I walked away.

Last week, Jeevan told me that on the day we met, he had decided that he despised me. His despise clearly didn't last very long.

A couple of days later, as I was sitting in the backyard letting my nails dry in the sun, my aunt Joti walked into the backyard with Jeevan at her side.

"Hey, Sahaara, this is Jeevan. He just moved into the neighborhood," she said.

"Umm . . . I know that already," I replied, suddenly feeling unbearably uncomfortable. His expression mirrored mine. He was in my territory now. He curled up his comic book in his hands.

"Well," my aunt replied slowly, sensing the tension between us, "I think you guys should hang out. Jeevan's mom wants him to make friends." She gave me the look that meant I shouldn't argue.

"Okay, Maasi Jee," I replied respectfully. Her expression relaxed. I think she was grateful that I didn't put up a fight. Mom had always taught me to call Joti "Maasi Jee" even though she wasn't my real aunt. Their family had taken Mom in when she had no one. Joti's mom would always be my bibi ji, my grandmother, even if I were to one day meet the woman who brought my mom into this world.

When she walked inside, I returned my attention to my nails and Jeevan sat down on a lawn chair, opening up his comic book. He eyed me as though waiting for a snide remark. Instead, the cover of his book caught my eye: there was a black woman with cornrowed hair soaring across the front page, with two very dangerous-looking women following behind her.

"You read books about girls?" I asked, slightly impressed.

"Yeah," he replied without looking up. "What's wrong with that?"

"I— Nothing. I think that's cool." It was my turn to be embarrassed now.

"Natasha Irons is way cooler than half the guys people like to read about, you know, considering that she beat the shit out of Steel." I had no idea who Steel was, but my surprise at the word *shit* was probably apparent on my face. Maybe he wasn't so lame, after all.

"Sorry . . . I was mean," I attempted awkwardly.

"Whatever," he replied with a whisper of a smile.

As I park my truck in the driveway of our house, I'm drawn out of my memories at the sound of my phone vibrating.

Sunny: What you up to tonight? Do you have time to hang out?

Sahaara: Picking up my mom from the SkyTrain. She's off work soon.

Sunny: What time are you grabbing her?

Sahaara: Around 11:30.

Sunny: ...

Sunny: We can chill then. Meet me at Boston Pizza?

Sahaara: Not hungry.

Sunny: Fine. Bear Creek Park?

I hesitate for a moment.

Sahaara: Ugh. Okay.

"So . . . everything cool with you?" he asks, his large almond eyes slipping in and out of the shadows as the swings carry us through the air.

"I've been all right." I don't want to tell him. I haven't seen him since the last day of school, and we stopped talking three months before that. It had been so easy to ignore him while I was distracted by the excitement of graduating. "How have you been?"

"I've been okay. Just been busy with work—"

"Work? At the restaurant or in Mani's basement?!" I say, cutting him off.

He looks at me sheepishly, offering no response to my question.

"Just okay, huh?"

"Yup." He goes quiet the way he usually does when he's lost in thought. He runs his Jordans against the ground to slow his swing to a halt. I do the same.

"You wanna talk about it?"

"It's just the usual shit. Dad started drinking again. Is there really a point in talking about it?"

My mom has always been distant in her own way. For reasons I'm still trying to understand. But I can't imagine what it's like dealing with an alcoholic parent. I hate that I don't know how to help.

"I'm sorry, Sunny."

"Why apologize? Not like it's your fault." He pauses again. "Let me push you."

"Go for it."

He pulls my swing as far as he can and then pushes me with

a force that I forgot exists in his lean body. I let myself feel the cold wind in my face, welcome after another far-too-hot summer day. After a few moments, I grab hold of his arm, trying to slow the momentum.

"Wanna see who can go higher?"

As I invest all my energy in winning, I look over to see a wide grin overtake him. It used to be so strange seeing him like this. Jaw softened and eyes filled with something other than disinterest. Actually having fun.

"What is this? Happiness? On Sunny Sahota's face?!"

"What?!" He laughs. "You act like I'm always miserable."

"You know you have serious resting bitch face, right? Like . . . you make Mr. Johnson seem like a teddy bear."

He erupts in laughter. "Holy shit. Do you remember the day I came in hella late and he made me run laps in the rain?"

"He was muttering about you under his breath when he came back in."

"I never told you this but when I finished running, he told me that he'd kick me off the basketball team if I came in late again. I tried to tell him why I was late, but he literally said that I'm full of shit. Aren't teachers not supposed to swear?"

"No . . . I don't think they are. But since when does that matter? Is that why you stopped playing basketball?"

"Nah. I got busy with other stuff. But, hold up. You noticed that I stopped playing?" His mouth forms that stupidly adorable grin.

"I was going to games for Jeevan, you jackass, not for you," I haughtily retort. "Don't flatter yourself."

He shrugs. Something shifts in the space between us at the mention of Jeevan's name.

"Is Jeevan good?"

"He is but . . . why don't you ask him yourself?"

Sunny shakes his head and laughs. "Yeah . . . don't think that's a good idea. Doesn't seem like he wants to hear from me."

"Can you blame him, though? Honestly, I dunno what you were thinking."

"Wait—what? I don't even know what I did."

I raise my eyebrows in disbelief. "How do you not know, Sunny? *Man up*? You told him to man up when he told you about his dad going to jail?"

"Oh. Yeah. But shit, man! He was crying! What was I supposed to do? Wipe his tears for him? This stuff isn't easy for anyone, and the sooner he realizes that, the better he'll be."

"You say that like you've never had to cry before. Like your dad—"

"Just leave it, man. Maybe I shouldn't have said that, but I don't think that's why he cut me out. He just needed a reason."

"Well . . . yeah. He's a protective friend. Again, can't really blame him."

"That's not . . . what I meant. But, okay. Is that even fair? This shit is complicated and . . . you knew I didn't want to be in a relationship. I just . . . I can't be with anyone."

I stare at the ground feeling a weird pang in my stomach. I know these things about him. All the ways it hurt when he would walk in and out. And yet, it always feels like a hook around my neck when he calls—I let the anchor pull me back in. Maybe it's because I know too much.

We both look down at our phones in silence.

"Sahaara, I'm sorry. I need to go. Lost track of time."

The corner of my phone screen tells me that it's 11:15 p.m.

"It's cool. I need to go, too. You heading home?" I ask.

"Nope." He sighs. "Work."

Raindrops gather on the windshield as I wait for Mom outside of the train station. My fingers itch for my phone but I refuse to text him first. As if on cue, my phone vibrates.

It's Jeevan.

Jeevan: How u feeling?

Sahaara: I don't know, honestly. Just trying not to think about everything.

Sahaara: My stomach is still in knots, though.

Jeevan: ☹

Jeevan: Like I said, we're gunna figure this out together. Right now, just try to breathe?

Sahaara: Trying.

The truth is, no matter what—or who—I try to distract myself with, nothing is working. Last Friday is always at the back of my mind. I was sitting in the living room with Bibi Jee when Mom and Joti Maasi stepped through the front door. Mom was silently shaking. I don't remember ever seeing Maasi so serious.

"What's going on?" I asked.

"So that lady—Gurinder—the red-haired lady—their family owns Daman's, right? She—she got into an argument with your mom and she —"

"She threatened to report me," whispered Mom, finishing Maasi's sentence.

"What? What does this mean? Report you? To the police?" my mind traveled to a thousand places at once.

Maasi nodded solemnly. "But I mean . . . why would she report an undocumented employee at her own restaurant? They'd obviously get in trouble, too, right?" She raised an important point. I exhaled. Maybe it would be okay.

Of course, none of us were sure what would happen. We're never sure. That's what I hate the most. The butterflies of anxiety never completely go away—they just die down sometimes.

Sahaara: Honestly, that aunty is so ridiculous. Who threatens to report an undocumented person just because they're mad about some petty argument?

Jeevan: Yup. So dumb. My mom knows her too, though. She said she just runs her mouth a lot. I wouldn't stress.

Sahaara: I know. But still. It just makes me so fkn angry that she would say something like that to my mom. Like someone else's life is a joke.

A part of me wants to cry, but my mom should be out of the station any minute. The last thing she needs right now is the sight of me sobbing over all this. I change the subject.

Sahaara: Anyways...don't kill me but I hung out with Sunny.

Jeevan: ...

Sahaara: He asked how you were doing

Jeevan: Lol. Did he bother asking how *you* are?

Sahaara: :/

Jeevan: Idk Sahaara. You already know what it is with him. But you do what you want.

Sahaara: What's that supposed to mean?

Jeevan: I'm sorry...that didn't come out right. I'm half asleep. Can we talk about this tomorrow?

Sahaara: Cool.

Jeevan begins to type. Oh God. It's a long message. I can feel irritation swelling within me even though I know he means well. I don't need a lecture right now. I just need a hug.

As I look up in exasperation, my breath falters. The whirring in my head, constantly reminding me of what must be done next, suddenly goes silent. Even the butterflies have stopped fluttering. The scene before me is in slow motion. It is a walk through a tidal wave. It is everything that I have ever feared. I forget how to breathe as I watch a uniformed police officer guide my mom into the back seat of his car.

"WHERE ARE YOU TAKING HER?!" comes a voice that feels detached from my body. I sprint across the parking lot as a car slams its brakes to avoid colliding with me. The sound of his car horn only exists in the distance.

"We have concerns about this woman's immigration status. We're holding her until CBSA arrives," replies the officer, with a voice that is far too calm for the moment that will shatter my world. Head downturned, she won't look at me. I'm not sure if it's because of pride or shame. In my mom's case, it may be the same thing.

I don't know when I began to cry but my words leave my mouth between sobs: "That's my mom. Can I talk to her? Can you open the window?"

The officer eyes me warily and then reaches inside to lower the window.

"Mom?" It's all that manages to escape my lips: the first word I learned and the only one that will ever matter. She turns her gaze toward mine and her eyes, so often guarded fortresses, fill with tears when they lock into mine. I watch as a lifetime of pain finally reveals itself across her face.

"I love you, Sahaara. It's going to be okay," she manages.

"How do you know that, Mom?"

"Just promise me you'll go to your class tomorrow." There's desperation in her voice. She's actually serious.

I laugh at the absurdity of this. Of everything. I laugh because I don't know what else to do.

"Okay."

he doesn’t know sunny like i do

i apologize when i get too close
i try to remember myself
when i forget that your walls are in place for a reason
but can you blame me for wanting
to take all this hurt & make water of it?
for thinking that if it finally poured from your eyes
you’d be free?

she doesn't know sunny like i do

will you love her
heart before hands before reason
like her mind is light and you've
never heard of sunglasses?

will you love her with eyes wide in wonder
as if her thoughts are an entire dance and
you are honored to have a front-row seat?

will you love her
like the word *commitment* is
a coin and your pockets are
overflowing with change?

will you love her with every sunflower
that blooms from your eyes
every planet that orbits
the expanse of your good intentions
every tree in the forest beneath your chest
that has patiently met sun and wind
thunder and rain?

will you love her the way we do
who have grasped her fingers
long before she emerged from
this cocoon?

if there is hesitation in your voice
i will hold her instead.

the idea scares the hell out of me. don't get me wrong. i see all the ways it could bloom. the way it could be an entire glittering mosaic draped across the walls of our bodies. but i also know all the ways it could shatter over our skin. and don't lie. you can see it, too. a million jagged pieces of glass pouring over us and into us. breaking us. and what would happen then? when we can't pick up our own pieces let alone each other's?

this friendship is this only thing that has ever held me. and if we held each other any closer maybe our fragility would overcome all our good intentions. and maybe it's selfish of me. to sense something just beneath your skin and still reach for you when my palms shake. maybe it's selfish. but you don't pull away, either.

sahaara x

dear mom

i know you worry about the way i worry
i know there are walls in places
where rivers want to flow
i know it feels like there is a clenched fist
beating beneath your chest sometimes
but i can hold your heart
just as you have held my hand
and maybe we will both unfurl
and maybe we will both blossom
beneath all this sunlight.

for kiran

here it is
                        your echoing heart.

all cement floors and faraway ceilings
all abandoned warehouse windows
and rusted metal gates
wedged open just wide enough
to let strangers in too easily

and you see shame
in the uninvited feet
that have rested here.
when you have gathered
all that life has given you
into the palm of a single hand to
craft your own broom and sweep.
when you have done your best
to push each door shut even if
the work has left you too tired
to ever open them again.

this.   all of this.
you have done on your own.
and the weight of that exists
in a place far deeper
than the scars.

heart (n)

a hollow muscle pumping blood throughout the body. roughly the size of a fist and capable of reaching into all spaces. in perpetual motion until it is not. creates its own electricity. brings its own flesh to life. moves in perfect synchronization with itself. except when things slip out of flawless order. then it calls for help. then the sparks need to come from elsewhere. and so interesting it is that when the current comes from outside, it stops the organ altogether. freezes everything. for a split second. in the hope that it will rekindle the thought of its own song.

funny how the heart is
associated with love.

i suppose there's something loving
about every cell of this body.

whole

i can still trace the softness
in your skin that you told me
turned to ash in the fire.

of course
they're drawn to your magic

you soar far above their heads
like peter pan

but that doesn't mean
you need to be refuge
for all these lost boys.

there are some wounds our hands can't stitch

my love
you wouldn't hold it against yourself
if you couldn't diagnose an illness
or offer a cure to every physical hurt that invades a body

so why do you break your own bones
when you can't heal their aching minds?
there are some things that are simply bigger than us
despite the way our intentions glitter with good meaning

it's okay. it's okay. it's okay.
please forgive yourself.

i am still searching for ways to not hurt that which i claim to love. i am still searching for ways to not hurt. for ways to love. for ways to know that i don't deserve to hurt for failing to love. for loving least of all myself. for loving in the wrong ways at the wrong time. for not knowing how to scrub my own bones clean of some love. love that has seeped through my skin and made a home in marrow that does not know all the sweetness it already contains. love that is an intruder within a body still learning to hold itself. to choose. to decide which love should have the house keys and which love has long overstayed its welcome. to love something more than electricity and an array of invisible, tangled strings. i am still searching for ways to be at peace. to find solace within a stillness that i am too afraid to speak to. in a place where stillness can teach the hurt how to wash itself away.

on the word *sorry*

so you messed up. you poured all your rage into a glass jar and smashed it against the tiles. yes, this was its unbecoming. yes, the jagged edges hurt. and yes, you then tried to piece it all back together with promises. but you know as well as i do, love, that whether you try to pour water or milk or sugar in it now, no matter how your intentions ache with all your regret, there is no adhesive strong enough to stop everything from slipping through the cracks.

i am not asking you to leave all your sadness on the ground and turn a blind eye to the way it hurts. or to dismiss the way your chest churns with guilt when your mind wanders back to this moment's bitter roots. i am simply asking you to accept that sometimes we cause irreversible pain to the people we hoped would never know anything like it and the only way to heal is to let yourself grow and the only way to say sorry is to mean that you are with all the decisions that you will make and the only way to truly be better is to put aside a selfish sadness, accept your humanity and look upon the ones you hold dear as made of skin and bone and glass.

in another life,
we bloom.
—pavana reddy

is there a way to forgive you without watching myself
vanish?

in a different life, we are whole and you are everything
i thought you were. there are no splinters in your voice
or contorted conditions upon this love. there are no refused
apologies or burning carcasses in place of the word *sorry.*
there are no stinging eyes. most of all, there are no marks.

in a different life, i do not imagine all the ways that silence
must stretch across space / measure the dimensions of a
room / fill every crevice / in order to keep me safe.

in a different life, you apologize for the little things,
like missing a performance or getting late for a get-together
and these are also the big things. i never grapple with
the thought that a world without you could exist before
this noiseless dam breaks.

i am told that forgiveness alone will free me
and instead i watch myself erode,
rock
to sand
to dust,
in every moment i am told to let go.

love does not leave bruises. across your arms or across your mind. love does not lend itself as an explanation. an excuse. love does not hollow out your flesh and call your aching shell selfless. love does not frighten or trap or suffocate. love does not justify or manipulate or seethe in anger. love does not apologize for the same crime every night because it's still learning how to stop. love does not force you to stay. love does not whisper all the reasons why no one else would ever want you. love does not convince you that the pain is for your own good. so when they say they only break you because of love, do not believe them.

love would never do that.

but don't you understand
how it hurt me?
doesn't that explain why
i do this to you? doesn't
that matter?

of course the pain matters.
but it's not a weapon that should
be pointed at anyone   least of all
those who you call loved ones.
the pain explains but
it doesn't justify.
it never justifies.

sometimes they will crave
your body and hate your mind.
it will be the kind of violence
that burns from the inside out.
before you find yourself
stitching the wounds back
together with your own
calloused fingers and
mistaking the patience
in the seams for love

find your own hand
hold it tight
and walk out the door.

you convince yourself that the stinging friction
between your bones is romantic.
as if this is the only way to kindle fire.
as if water cannot sparkle while it quenches thirst.

empty

if i could
i think i would
pull all the need
out of me.
to be heard.
to be loved.
to be needed.
by something
that is not
already embedded
in my own bones.
but instead i am here.
and human. and somehow
made up of less skin than glass.
transparent about that which
i (do not) contain.

leave for good

no matter how many times
you are drawn back to this
burning house   fire will not
meet you with kindness.

if he is the place where
your head rests each night
but he is never the place
where the poems arise
perhaps you shouldn't
call this home.

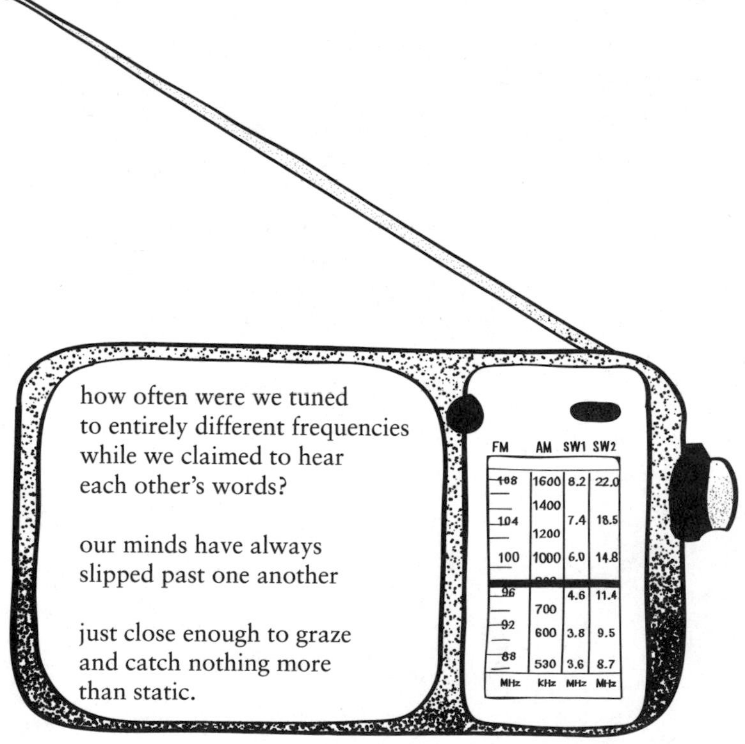

how often were we tuned
to entirely different frequencies
while we claimed to hear
each other's words?

our minds have always
slipped past one another

just close enough to graze
and catch nothing more
than static.

sometimes
no matter how hard you try
the soil just isn't right
and the water goes nowhere
but downward.

even the most carefully planted seeds
cannot flourish where they were never
meant to stay.

there are all sorts of braveries in this world
& maybe this could sit small in a field among them

instead of asking this love again

& again

& again

& again

to stretch further than its fabric will allow
what if you set it down?

what is the worst that could happen
if you no longer clung to this ill-fitting coat?

no, it was nothing like removing a coat. it was like peeling off my own skin and waiting for the cells to regenerate. staying was the only other thing that felt so counterintuitive. that felt both terribly right and wrong.

then you left
just like i asked you to
& my body was just a body
my skin just a shell
my heart just a valve
& all the magic just a
story i wrote by myself

some poems
are water

some poems flow
only from the eyes.

after all this time
you hold back the tide
behind your eyes
thinking i cannot
swim.

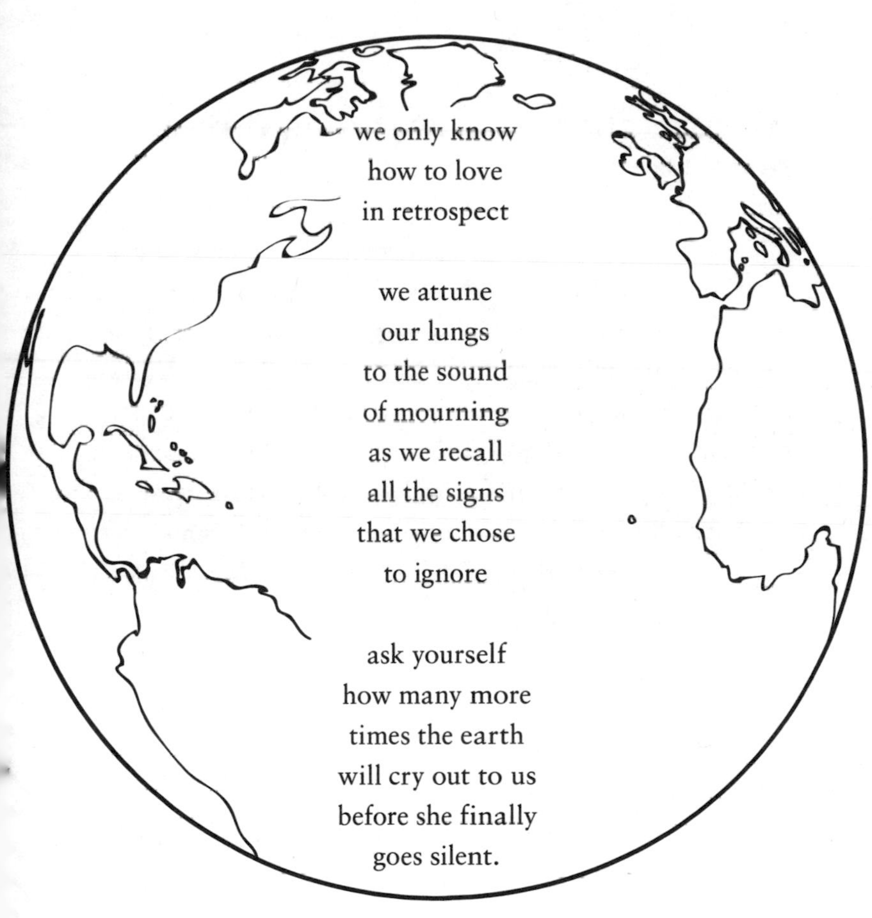

we only know
how to love
in retrospect

we attune
our lungs
to the sound
of mourning
as we recall
all the signs
that we chose
to ignore

ask yourself
how many more
times the earth
will cry out to us
before she finally
goes silent.

we cross the global warming threshold in 2036

in the dream, we were on a planet that could no longer give birth to our children. in the dream, the sun was inching closer to our faces and our skin was patiently waiting. in the dream, the ocean came to us. met us at our necks because we never came when she called for help. in the dream, we met a woman whose mother died (she said she held my poems in her hands). in the dream, we held each other close because that's what humans do—hold everything until it is no longer within our grasp. in the dream, i remembered that i couldn't hold you close enough to keep you.

the poem will not immortalize us.
it will not horcrux us into
something more
than blood
and marrow
and bone
eventually the poem will
disintegrate into the earth
and the earth will disintegrate
into the universe and the universe
will disintegrate into silence

and the poem
while it is here
will do what it is
meant to do —

teach us to move as a river
that can weave life and feel
and softly let go.

family

i don't love in strategically
poured increments. when i love,
i love hard. i leave no space for
question. i place the full contents
of my mind on the table. it's all
here for you to see and hear
and run from because there is
no need to be eased into the
parts of my being that
aren't so soft to the touch.

and that is why
when you come for the poems.
i let you sit within the full
cavern of my voice. let you
feel the walls shake and know
what it is to light fire within
frigid cold. and if after all this.
you still want to stay. how can
i call you anything less than
my own?

a woman once offered me a pencil
& i thanked her profusely

another offered me life
again & again
& i never got around
to thanking her.

if i should have a son

i.
i will teach him that manhood is not
in the number of needless sighs he
can withdraw but in the way his light
reflects off those his intentions
shine upon

ii.
i will remind him that a woman's body
is not a storage house for his insecurities
nor her mind a cheap canvas where his
oil-paint words can prepare a draft for
the next mural

iii.
i will show him that fear is not love and
that love is not fear: instilling fear has more
to do with cowardice than respect even
when it feels otherwise

iv.
when his sadness is stifled by the silence
this world has taught him to seek shelter beneath
i will show him that the weight of the world does
not rest upon his aching shoulders nor his hardened
fists although walls seem to understand us better
than humans sometimes.

v.
i will raise him to be the type of being who
knows that manhood does not have to be
an unyielding facade put on for an audience
but a softness. a stillness. a wakefulness.
in knowing one's self.

homage to sarah kay's
"if i should have a daughter"

fourth grader

she kneels beside the creek
pours a salmon fry into the water
and refuses to let go of my hand
until she is at a safe distance from
the water's edge

at some point in the day
she will tell me that she hates
every subject at school except art
that i should only teach her how to
paint stories and mix shades of
turquoise and magenta to take
home to her mother

we are learning about refugees
in social studies
she hears the words *bomb*
and *escape* and *water*
and for the first time
tells me that she is from
either syria or iraq
unsure which home
she ran from first

her hand finds mine
holds tight for fear of the water
holds tight because she does not
know whether the waves can
return to swallow her.

the english professor
quotes another dead white man
asks us whether it is better to
have loved and lost than
to have never loved at all

the shaheeds stand before me
hearts and bodies still intact
hands tied behind their backs
with the crowns once tied
around their heads

one by one they are
washed away by the river

red blooms
where life once was
and love blooms
where the earth loses
her beloveds.

to shaheed jaswant singh khalra
to every singh and kaur whose
extrajudicial murder was
uncovered by his work

i think it might be true that we spend our lives
seeking our first loves within the ones who
follow because all this time i have been waiting
for the sight of my guru behind human eyes.

guru nanak

you tell me to find
something that is real
and i tell you
that i am hurting
and you tell me to hold
something that is real
and i tell you
that i am hurting
and you tell me to love
something that is real
and i tell you
that i am hurting
and you tell me to keep
something that is real
and i tell you
that i am hurting
and

the memory of skin

on these unexpected occasions
the deep intones of a man's voice
doors closed too heavily and hastily
footsteps creaking close to these uninsulated walls
turn her body into an unstill
    jagged thing seeking shelter.

and she must remind herself
that no one is going to break the lock
that the person who opens the door
has hands softer than still water
that her body is wise enough
to remember all the stories
that will keep her safe
that her chest is pounding
because her heart loves her
enough to do its best to
protect her.

moonlight moves in waves
through the darkened alleys
beneath my chest
illuminated by your love.

i’ve being trying for years to bring it to the table.
to redirect its attention. make it see reason.
to have a constructive conversation about all the good
we could do if we were on the same side. but my heart has
a will of its own and only ever speaks to me through
a clenched jaw and tearful eyes. it’s rarely had ears for me
and i’m a shitty negotiator anyways. i somehow always
listen long enough to forget my own point.

tbh i'm just scared that this
empty space inside me
will only ever be shaped like you

[delete for everyone] [you deleted this message]

(love) language barrier

how much beauty is abandoned
because there is no time
to decipher something
that seems so unfamiliar?

how much love is lost in translation
because we are still learning
to communicate in a new language?

we met at the edges of ourselves
broken down, weather-worn minds
and bodies clothed so deceptively in youth

we met at the peripheries of ourselves
pushed out of our own skins
by all the demons that had settled
comfortably in our
wakeful hazy thoughts

and yet somehow
you and all your closeness
me and all my questions
we and all our tangled stories
became a road map deciphered together
where we learned the art of
tracing our steps backward
to find our way home.

you
are neither river nor sun
neither moon nor light

you are too present
in this skin to be held
by a metaphor.

when we met i was graced with no elaborate
metaphors except that you seemed imaginary
until you were right before me
like the distant expiry date on this passport
immaterial but inevitable.

when i leave
please scour each jammed cupboard for your smile
because somehow we shared the earth
at the exact same moment
because the poems wouldn't come
until i closed my eyes to think of you
because between all these hands
i managed to take hold of yours
and what a stunning accident that was.

sincerity

surround yourself with those
who would be there without
a piece of you to stand upon

those who are drawn to
your highest self

those who wish to stand
by your side as you plant
roots in soil far richer than
hatred or praise.

suffocating

the flowers
on the windowsill
face the sun.
                    not me.
they need light more
than i need to see them.

perhaps the same principle applies
with the ones we love.

only you can teach
your insides to bloom
but i will
stay here,
as long as
you may need,
with water

when i ran from my own heart

do not break from your people
no matter the temptation
no matter the ease
life flows from the roots
of your sister
to the veins of your mother
to the synapses of your elders
to the leaves of your son
to you
and a severed branch
cannot bear fruit.

i ask why you come to me with honey-sweet words
and you remind me that last week, i told you i was breaking.
you think that maybe   just maybe
something sticky could help put my pieces back together

they say lavender softens anxiety
and i wonder whether i can
plant a garden so dense
in your mind
that the knots in your chest unravel
and never tighten again.

accidental poems

1. secure your own mask before helping others
2. the shoreline erasing everything we draw
3. a first grader offering the front of the line to someone else
4. objects in mirror are closer than they appear
5. my mother asking incessantly if I have eaten
6. the fish greeting their reflections in glass
7. please mind the gap between the train and the platform
8. how she blinks back tears when she encounters kindness
9. the moon reaching into the sky before the sun sets
10. your hand somehow finding mine in the dark

your eyes are an ocean.
there i said it & i suppose i'm not
supposed to feel that way. but can you
blame me? when they sing in such a
sun-consuming way. when they pour gentle
rivers in place of poems. when they offer me
every reason to wonder by making sense of all
the light. when they remind me of all the beauty
embedded in brown. i drown in your eyes again
& again & feel all the guilt befitting a woman
like me whose most secret love is herself.

a note to self:

you are worth every moment
that led you to yourself

you're the one i'd choose
every single time.

i love knowing that it will hurt. the words sit and echo for a moment.

they shake the past from its place on the shelf and i watch all my fears fall to the floor. i would have sooner made you hate me than face the fact that we would one day be pulled apart. love this full and dense made me queasy. so i set fire to the thought of us. dropped us from skyscraper rooftops. put us in a boat to nowhere and pushed us far from the shore. made you see all the reasons why this would sting and added hurt for authenticity.

call it cowardice. call it humanness. this hardened cement that would not allow me to grow.

light (n)

a natural agent that renders objects visible to the eye. wave and particle. simultaneously and one at a time. travels faster than most else in the universe. beaten maybe just by quantum entanglement and negative matter and nothing. capable of reaching through water. in the form that makes sense to us, at least. reflects. warms. overwhelms. bewilders. leaves no secrets. wraps itself around all directions and weightlessly holds. fills. teaches me in its absence. outlines each space it has not reached and saves it for later. once said to travel through ether. often said to be found at the ends of tunnels. so often imagined as more. more than photon. more than electromagnetic wave. only reveals itself in the form that i am looking for.

where in the body do you
think light would be seated?

i'd like to imagine
everywhere.

the fever needed to swelter
the womb needed to contract
the heart needed to know
growing pains

the body has
never crafted life
without first feeling it.

joy isn't always linear

i feel my heart
rise in the morning and set at night
trace its journey across an entire sky
& watch it cast shadows as long as its light

i know my heart to illuminate my body in cycles
and remember that this, too, is nature.

the thoughts that withhold sleep
from you within the stillest hours
are the ones that should be carried
into the morning.

joyful or painful
they demand resolution
only light can offer.

be easy with yourself. with your healing. know that this journey will very often look more like hills and valleys than a paved road. go within. find all the flowers and still water tucked beneath your chest. abandon this shivering hypermasculinity that the colonizer placed in the hands of our men. it has never fed us like the sweetness of community. of meditation. nourish all the tulips and dahlias sitting inside you. they can still grow here after all this. let sunlight into the garden of your brother's mind. tend kindly to your own. know what you need and don't be afraid to ask for it. if you need a shoulder. if you need listening ears. if you need a friend to sit beside you until the sun rises. know that there's someone. always someone. who wants to be here. it's impossible, isn't it? for all these people to have all this love and for none of it to be for you. believe in that. if only for the time it takes for us to reach you. so long as there is air dancing in and out of this body, there is a way—some way—for us to flourish.

when you shrink as you enter a room these are the things that cross my mind

1. have you ever heard yourself laugh?
it always forces me to do the same.
your laughter makes contagious things
seem beautiful.

2. you are light and even the shadows
you cast are warm.

3. how long has it been since you stopped
to marvel at the entire garden of your thoughts?
i swear, sometimes orchids fall when you speak.

4. the rain inside me was unrelenting.
you didn't need to. you really didn't.
but you offered me an umbrella.

5. i don't think you saw my eyes
the night your work was on display.
the room was far too dark.
they were filled with water.

6. if it was me, you would demand
that i climb my mountain.
today, i'm asking you to face yours.

7. you make me feel like i matter.
that's a big deal for someone like me.

8. i've been searching for a mirror capable of reflecting
your joy. i guess this normal one will have to do for now.
remember that you are a universe and this single surface
cannot contain you.

9. i know it's impossible to be okay just by
touching the hearts of others. not when everything
inside you stings. but you helped someone else heal.
that came from within you. imagine what you could do
to nourish your own heart.

10. i can't count how many times a day
you choose to be your most honest self.
when this room tells you to shrink
remind it of your blooming.

i tell myself that my body
is a garden of flowers
but when most of us
are caught up
in the scent of roses
we forget about the dirt
that they bloom from

all the struggle
that comes before the sunlight
all the push that pulls us
to stay rooted in ourselves

and here we are. finding ourselves.
as we crack and grow
and rise.

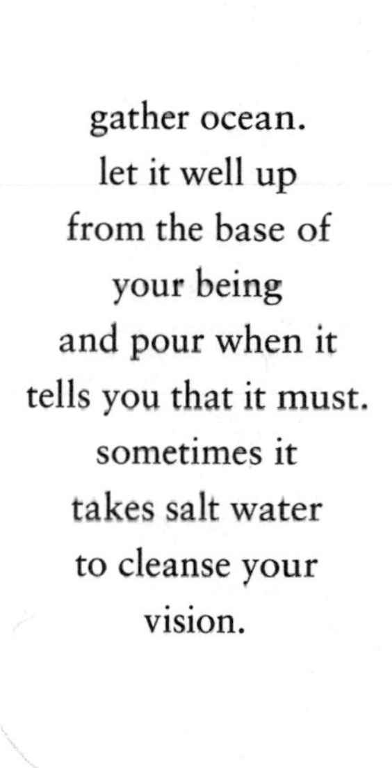

gather ocean.
let it well up
from the base of
your being
and pour when it
tells you that it must.
sometimes it
takes salt water
to cleanse your
vision.

i am tired of teaching resilience
to brown babies who have already
seen enough to find brick walls
in all the places where joy should be.

today, the talk on alcoholism is canceled.
we don't say the word *depression* but we
cope in song-filled ways. today, there is
no mention of a drunk dad or a hurting
mom or a gunshot in the place of a
beating heart.

today, they teach me how to build
on minecraft. how a universe can be crafted
from nothing but imagination. how to find
refuge in the things adults throw away.
how to face an overwhelming world
with a fresh set of eyes.

the earth aches when hardened soil
cracks open but this is the only way
to anchor new roots

my people have never silenced pain
but we have always honored that
which allows us to grow.

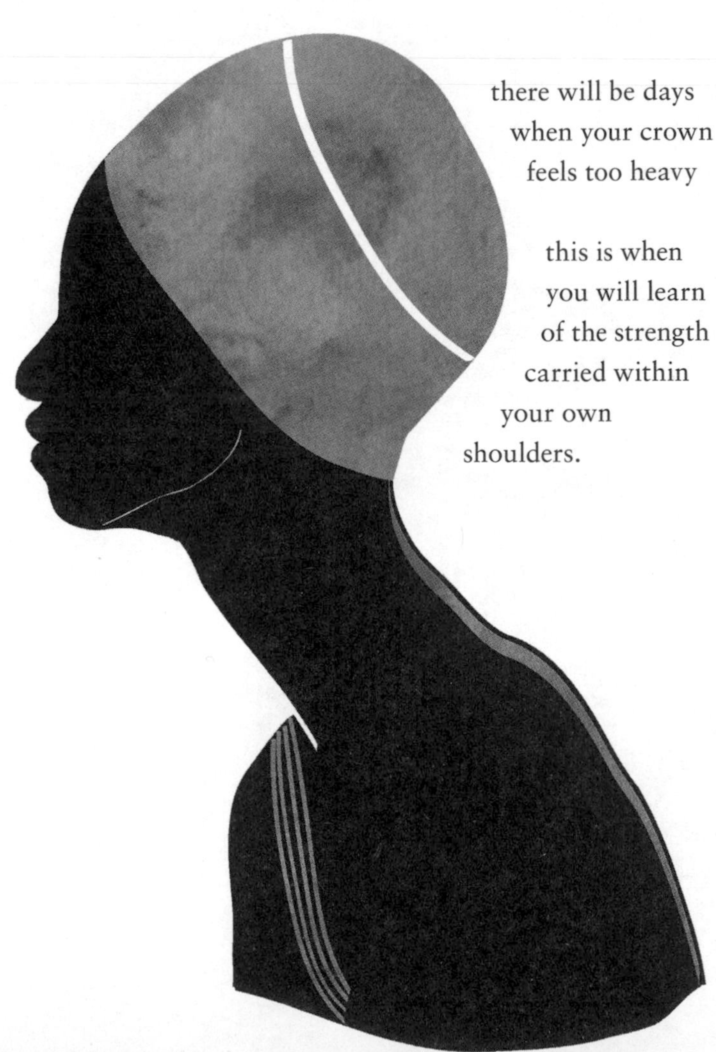

there will be days
when your crown
feels too heavy

this is when
you will learn
of the strength
carried within
your own
shoulders.

i know what my body wants.   but do i know what i want?   i'm trying to tell myself   that there's a difference. that the layers of me are bound together but never fused.   that my eyes are not always my nerves are not always my heart is not always my brain is not always the electricity beneath my skin is   not always   my soul.

i meditate to send earth back to earth. water back to water. air back to air.   i am the weaving of an entire universe. this means that i can also be unraveled.

this morning, i wake up as if something wants me.
i take another breath because i've been searching for
too long for a reason to breathe.
call it the universe. call it the divine. call it whatever.
but i know i was created by something
much larger than a human form.
i know this body, a city of its own,
is the eighth wonder of the world.
i know that every breath i take defies
too many probabilities to count.
i know that i'm hardly here long enough
to unravel the mess of it all.

but this morning, i wake up as if life herself wants me
because, maybe, it's true.

this is how i remember to want myself.

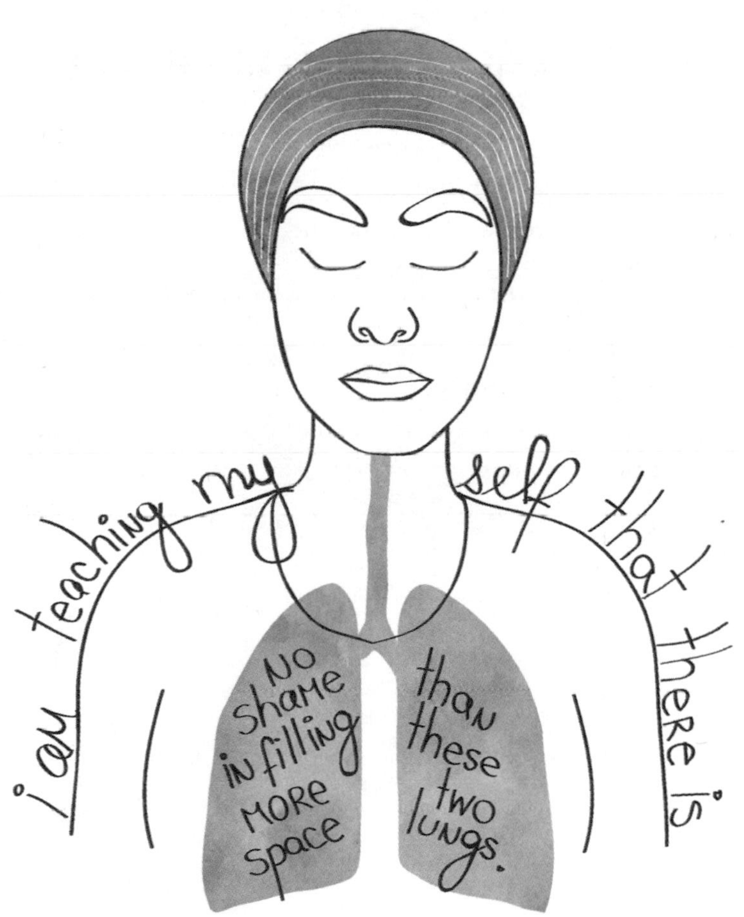
i am teaching myself that there is
no shame in filling more space
than these two lungs.

if it didn't expand exactly like this

you are the most unlikely outcome
of the most unlikely universe.
the place where atoms and wonder met.
gathering into
muscle and heart
nerve and skin
lungs and light.

you are overwhelming.

i have never known a living thing
to remain completely still

time asks my body to change
and i ask myself to be okay with it
you say my skin is not the type to wrinkle
with old age and i wonder whether trees
lose their beauty with each ring.
you say my hair is too pronounced
and i wonder whether flowers would
cry if they saw one too many petal.
you say my waist is to your liking today
but that life will catch up to me one day.

and i look all the way to the end
when a tall sequoia tree will fall to the ground
its roots pulled from the earth
its body sunken into land
its skin   still   somehow
a place where life can come home.

dear body,

a day will come when the work you have done so thanklessly will tire you. in this moment, for the first time in a very long time, i will see you. i will suddenly gaze deeper into self than these eyes have ever allowed and know that each part of this form is an impossibility. that i am not just mind encapsulated in motionless shell but rather an ever-moving world wandering another ever-moving world. it is only when you are breaking down that i will stop to meet the breath that escapes these lungs and feel the way a human can be filled up with something so small it is mistaken for nothing. you, nothing larger than cosmic dust to space, too insignificant for my own love but enough for the earth to want back. you, who moves blood through veins in silence. grows gentle garden upon skin in silence. sparks motion and breath and thought in silence. sustains this fragile, hopeful consciousness in silence. i speak to you as if we've always known each other. as if you weren't the one who introduced me to myself. as if you owe me a forever for bringing me here without first seeking my permission.

the truth is this.

you have done more than i will ever understand. and when the day comes when your selflessness in the face of my selfishness has exhausted you, i will go with you in peace. let all your water return to ocean. let all your air return to sky. i will let this listening universe do with you, in its wisdom, what i could not in my ego.

ਚਲਣਹਾਰ / *chalanhaar* / *transient*

i ask you to recall that this body is a short-term lease. no matter how tensely you hold on, it will eventually let go. *i* will go. *you* will go. so here we are. in these fractions of moments called our lives. in forms that are at once everything and nothing. in hearts that have already promised not to be ours.

how do we make this second of consciousness worthwhile?

how strange it is that i have clung to myself
in nothing but fear while only half-wakeful
only a sliver of moon

yet in those wordless moments scattered
so rarely across this human existence
when the entire expanse of my mind
sees and loves and feels and is
i am okay with leaving knowing
with conviction what it is to have lived.

in one breath

like all these lowercase letters strung together
as if they are the middle of a sentence and never the
beginning i am a continuation of every beautiful accident
that cultivated this universe this body has been gathered in
pieces from every being that came before me this mind has
been shaped by the rivers that my people traversed this air
wandering in and out of my form has traveled an entire earth
how can i not be overwhelmed by the way i am nothing more
than a piece of everything

the ancestors

i know very little about all the women who carved
lines into my palms but i do know what i am capable
of. i know which words taste like warm kheer and
which work has gone off. i know how to gaze at my
own skin without shrinking. i know that i can climb
a mountain without letting fear get the best of me.
i know that my imagination is old and instinctual
honest in ways that cannot be taught

i reach out across the cliff's edge and gaze into the
eyes of every past self still hovering in the
uncontained space of memory. i sit down at the
bottom of the valley and greet a face that the earth
has offered me this time. i imagine a woman with
eyes as round and unforgiving as mine. as outraged
at this world's cruelty as my grandmother. as giving
as my mother. unsure of whether anyone loves her
other than her own daughter. i imagine a young girl
running barefoot through rusty dirt rising
scattering dancing through humid air.
feeling something honest in her gut whispering that
joy should never be replaced with the word *honor.*

i imagine all the women i came from the way a
young girl might remember me one day. she will
paint stories with the tips of her fingers and perhaps
never reach the naked truth but she will know
what she is capable of because of the way she can
dream about each of her past selves.

there is something divine
in the way my sister's
identity exists within mine.
about the way our stories
and struggles and joys
are woven through one
another's although our
eyes may never have met

we carry each other.
just as we all carry
the name kaur.

when the dam breaks

solidarity is a water
that somehow flows over
and under and through
the cement of their borders.

migrant mother

you who dared to meet the earth
on the wrong side of the wall
you who led a delicate hand
to a place your tongues
are still learning to call home

you are living proof
that we can erase all the lines
they draw to cross us out.

before day breaks
they begin to dig
their borders
into our skin

at dawn they burn
in white-hot rage
when we rise
regardless.

what if

funny how you find
yourself here once again.
at the edge of the riverbed.
knowing that you cannot swim.
knowing that you cannot help
but dip your feet in the water.
certain that there is so much more
just beyond the safety of soil.

this page is for you
(yes, you.)

and fill their absence

with a poem gifted to yourself

interlude

right now, i am okay. right now feels like honeyed sunlight pouring into a quiet room. like seafoam curling around my ankles and all the butterflies in my stomach finally at rest. like every field in punjab watered and flourishing. like each cell in my body waking up to sing. like going home and not being afraid. i just thought you should know. i mean, remember. because i'm sure it won't always feel like this. but i don't want you to forget that this moment was possible. it can happen again.

and again.

she burnt
language
& let them

inhale the
incense.

why write something that you're
already running from? why paint
something that doesn't keep you up
at night? we don't half-heartedly
love, so why half-heartedly create?

know that this dizzying work
doesn't need to be universal. it
doesn't need to sacrifice identity
for appeal or melanated skin for
ears. your metaphors don't need to
be watered down and your
brushstrokes don't need to follow a
trajectory that was never yours to
begin with.

this art spans far beyond image.

it has the potential to heal you. to
break you. to expand you. to birth
a new you. your work. your heart.
mean so much more than the
hollow gaze of a hollow audience.

love, the way your art draws air
into your own lungs has always
been reason enough.

when the poems come

there is no middle ground.

i must either scrape the words
off the walls
painstakingly
carefully
one
by
one
    until they willfully walk

or they come to me in whirlpool
                a mess of metaphors
nearly too tangled to decipher
all at once
all beautiful
all aurora and citrus and lava
held together by nothing but
a river of sound.

i have no desire
for words that float
on water

i want language so thick
it will drown me with it.

fold the
unfinished
poems of
our people
into paper
lanterns and
release them

let light fill
all the spaces
where words
cannot yet go.

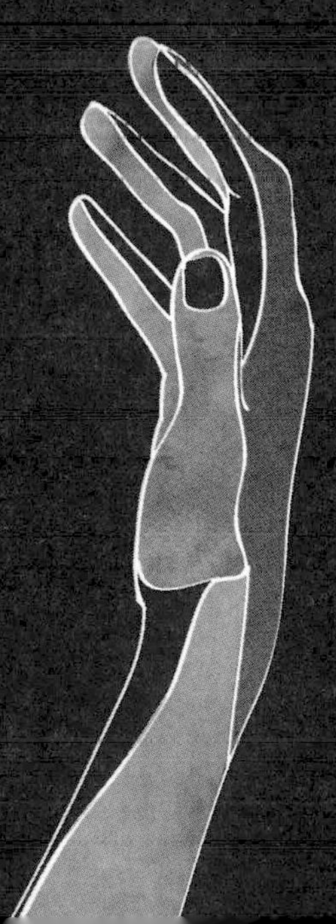

notes

page 3, this neighborhood

This poem responds to the way in which the primarily Punjabi West Abbotsford community is stigmatized. While gang violence in the West Abbotsford/Townline Hill area has made provincial headlines in British Columbia, the resilience, beauty, and hope planted within this young immigrant community goes painfully ignored.

page 8, ਪੱਕਾ ਰੰਗ / *pakka rang* / ripened color

Pakka rang or "ripened color" is a Punjabi phrase, often used derogatorily, that refers to dark skin. Its use, and the demonization of dark skin among South Asian communities, is arguably a product of internalized racism, resulting from the European colonization of South Asia. Prior to European colonization, terms such as *saaval* (ਸਾਂਵਲ), meaning dark-complexioned lover, were used to celebrate the beauty of dark skin.

page 17, the ideal sikh girl

This poem explores the way that *amritdhari* (baptized) Sikh girls and women are often subject to scrutiny from other Sikhs in relation to their physical appearance, perceived modesty and *kes* (uncut hair kept by Sikhs as a means of honoring the divinity of one's body).

page 22, my name is not sheila

"My name is not sheila" refers to a lyric in Sunidhi Chauhan and Vishal Dadlani's song "Sheila Ki Jawani." "Munni badnaam hui" refers to the title of Mamta Sharma and Aishwarya Nigam's song.

page 86, all this went down at once

Both historically and in present time, some South Asian families prefer the birth of boys over girls. This is, perhaps, due to patriarchal traditions of carrying on the family name and passing down wealth through sons. The mother-in-law described in the first stanza of this poem is one such person, finding value in the birth of her granddaughter by commenting that "at least her skin is fair."

page 91, trilokpuri

TrilokPuri refers to a neighborhood in East Delhi that was attacked during the anti-Sikh pogroms of November 1984. In response to the assassination of Prime Minister Indira Gandhi, thousands of Sikhs across Delhi and Punjab were targeted, tortured, and killed by angry mobs over the course of two horrific days.

page 177, the poem will not immortalize us

In this poem, I reference Horcruxes, as imagined by J. K. Rowling in the Harry Potter series. A Horcrux is a magical object that contains a fragment of a person's soul and makes them immortal.

page 183, to shaheed jaswant singh khalra

Jaswant Singh Khalra was a Sikh human rights activist who

"uncovered thousands of disappearances, unlawful killings and secret cremations of Sikhs, perpetrated by Punjab police" according to human rights organization Ensaaf. In 1995, he was abducted, tortured, and murdered by Punjab police because of his work. In 2005, six Punjab police officials were convicted for Khalra's murder.

page 214, i am tired of teaching resilience

I wrote this poem during my first year as a fourth-grade teacher. I was heartbroken by the traumatic experiences that some of my young students shared with me and worked to facilitate mental-health workshops for them. I found that sometimes the greatest healing came through play, the consistency of our classroom routines and creating a safe space to learn.

page 220, if it didn't expand exactly like this

The title of this poem is inspired by the scientific Big Bang theory. When I was younger, I remember being wonder-struck when I learned that the universe could have simply collapsed into itself as a black hole if it had expanded any differently during the Big Bang. It could have had the consistency of soup and life wouldn't have been possible. I found this both amazing and overwhelming. When I question my worth, I recall the wondrousness of the universe, as Carl Sagan might have.

page 227, carry the name kaur

The word *kaur* (ਕੌਰ), derived from the word *kuwar*, meaning "prince" or "next in line for the throne" is the last name given to all Sikh women in place of a traditional last name. All Sikh women take on the name Kaur as a means of celebrating spiritual identity and challenging the casteism inherent in traditional South Asian last names. By taking on the last name Kaur, Sikh women are no longer bound to the caste of their familial last name. Sikh men take on the last name Singh (ਸਿੰਘ).

i am infinitely grateful for

ishaval and rupi, who saw the value in this work when i could not see myself

nikki, jasjit, damanpreet, damneet, and ishleen, who read through all my drafts and brought this book home to itself

arjun and jaiden, whose feedback and humor mean the world

michelle superle and andrea macpherson at the university of the fraser valley, whose guidance made this work possible

sukhpreet singh, tasha kaur, jiwanjot kaur, priyanka kosanam, mette edith, melanie matining, and jessica zucker, whose time, input, and professional insights shaped my storytelling

katherine latshaw and tara weikum, who did more than they will ever know when they helped me place this piece of my heart in your hands

you

A stunning sequel of feminism, empowerment, and love.

Jasmin Kaur

returns with

IF I TELL YOU THE TRUTH.

HARPER

An Imprint of HarperCollins*Publishers*

www.epicreads.com